WONDER LIGHT

UNICORNS OF THE MIST

R.R. Russell

sourcebooks
jabberwocky

Published by Sourcebooks Jabberwocky, an imprint of Sourcebooks, Inc.
P.O. Box 4410, Naperville, Illinois 60567-4410
(630) 961-3900
Fax: (630) 961-2168
www.jabberwockykids.com

Library of Congress Cataloging-in-Publication data is on file with the publisher.

Source of Production: Versa Press, East Peoria, Illinois, USA
Date of Production: February 2014
Run Number: 5000746

Printed and bound in the United States of America.
VP 10 9 8 7 6 5 4 3 2 1

For my daughter. You're a fighter, Lahna.

April

CHAPTER 1

KEELY TURNED OFF THE ignition and pointed at the haunted island. "Well, Twig," she said, "there it is."

Mist swirled around the island in circles of warning. Spirals of rain and wind and secrets seemed to say, *If you come, Twig, we will break you on our rocks like the waves.* No one had lived on Lonehorn Island in recent memory, until the Murleys—and now a bunch of unwanted girls. Soon Twig would join them.

The wind whooshed from the island to shore and beat at the car windows with new fistfuls of rain. *We are the Island. Leave us alone, Twig, or we will snap you.*

Well, Keely would certainly get her way then. Keely said Twig's name as if she wished Twig would snap in two. Twig had liked her name, back when Daddy called her *Twig* as though he were certain one day she'd sprout leaves of pure gold. Now Daddy said her name like she was already broken. Now Daddy wasn't there, and Twig wouldn't be around when he came home.

A small, bright blue boat pulled up to the dock in front of the parking lot. A man in worn jeans and a dark green raincoat climbed out and tossed a line onto the dock. He paused to wave before tying down, and Keely smiled stiffly and waved back.

Then Keely looked at Twig, her resolve visibly softening. "Maybe I should come with you. The Murleys said it would be all right."

Twig shook her head firmly.

"Okay." The edge returned to Keely's voice. "Let's go meet Mr. Murley. Looks like he's got one of the other girls with him. Maybe you two can get to know each other on the way. Make friends." *You'd better, Twig*, her tone said. *You'll be there for a long, long time.*

Twig glared at the boat, at the small face pressed up against the window of the cabin. She got out and gave her car door a good slam. The rain lightened into fine, misty drops.

Twig ought to have been glad to get out of the car. The

three-hour drive north along the Washington coast to Cedar Harbor had been cold and dark and quiet. But thinking about Lonehorn Island made her want to jump right back in the car and beg her stepmother to take her home.

The little island in the distance was one of many scattered off the rocky coast beyond Cedar Harbor, but it was the only haunted one.

CHAPTER 2

"Put your hood up, Twig." There was a new tremble in Keely's voice as she pulled her own hood on tight.

Normally, Twig would've left her hood off just because Keely had told her to put it on. Left her head out so the rain could turn her long blond tangles dark with the wet. But Lonehorn Island made her shiver, so she pulled on the hood of her new, too expensive, all-weather jacket.

Keely had bought Twig new clothes too. "Good, sturdy farm clothes" she'd insisted Twig would need, and she'd stuffed the biggest suitcase Twig had ever seen full of them. Further evidence that Keely intended to be rid of her for good.

This morning Twig had ignored the new outfit her step-mom had chosen for her and dressed in her usual: a pair of boy's jeans from the Goodwill that had never fit her right; a

T-shirt of Mom's that hung to her knees, and whose peeling logo had once read "Tipperary Tavern"; the canvas shoes that only still fit because the toes had split open.

Twig zipped the zipper all the way up so that the jacket covered her mouth. She Velcroed a strip that tightened the fit. She was a turtle, eyes and nose poking out, the rest of her hidden. Her skinny, useless hands found the pockets, and they were warm. It wasn't so bad, this shell, even if it was bright red.

Keely struggled to pull the suitcase out of the trunk. Twig made no move to help; it wasn't *her* suitcase. Everything that was really hers was in the mini-backpack under her jacket, inside her shell like the rest of her, safe from everything cold and spitting and whipping around her.

Mr. Murley's work boots slap-thumped on the wet dock. He wasn't what Twig had expected a rich guy whose uncle had left him an entire island to be like. His jeans had a clean but rumpled look. The wind whooshed his hood off his gray-brown hair, and he left it down so that they could see his smile.

"Hold on there!" he called. "I'll give you a hand with that!"

"That's all right!" Keely slammed the suitcase against

the trunk several times before jerking it out and dropping it to the concrete.

She caught the handle in time to make sure it landed upright, on its wheels, but not in time to keep it from splashing into a puddle and spattering her pressed jeans. She fought with the handle until it extended, and she bump-jerked it to the dock behind her. Mr. Murley hurried to tie off the boat and come to their assistance, but Keely was quick and determined—determined to get rid of Twig.

"Good to see you again, Mrs. Tupper," Mr. Murley said. Keely had come last week, without Twig, to check the place out. "And you must be Twig." Mr. Murley held out his hand.

Twig looked at it, then back at her soppy socks sticking out of her shoe holes. Her stomach lurched. Mr. Murley squeezed her shoulder instead.

"Mrs. Tupper, you're welcome to come along to help Twig get settled in."

Twig looked up. "No," she said sharply.

Keely jumped. Twig hadn't said a word in three days. Not that she talked much at all since Daddy had left.

Twig grabbed the suitcase handle, not because it was hers, but because it was what was keeping them standing here, on the dock, instead of driving away in the boat—away from all hope of escape and all risk of breaking down and begging Keely to change her mind. Keely didn't want her; Twig didn't fit in Daddy's new family, and that was that.

Mr. Murley let Twig drag the suitcase over to the boat, but he picked it up when she stopped at the edge of the dock and stared down into the gap of black water that wanted to swallow her up. It was protecting the island, protecting its secrets, just like the mist that was the island's shell. The island wanted to be left alone. Twig's held-back shudder escaped. She knew how the island felt. *I'm sorry,* she said to the island, to its ghosts. *I have no choice.*

The rain thickened. The wind tore at her hood.

"I'll stay the night here in town." Keely nodded at Cedar Harbor behind her. "I'll be right here."

"I'll come get you in the morning." Mr. Murley hefted the suitcase into the boat. "Like we talked about. And bring you to the island so you can see how Twig's doing before you head home."

Mr. Murley regarded the enormous suitcase, then the little cabin door. It would be impossible to cram it through. He pushed it to the back of the boat instead and wrapped a tarp around it.

Keely squeezed Twig tight before she could duck away. "If you change your mind," she whispered quickly, "in the morning, I'll take you back home."

Twig twisted out of Keely's arms. Keely sniffed and pulled a tissue from her pocket. The rain got it thoroughly soggy before it even made it to her nose.

"Good-bye, sweetie!"

The boat rocked a little when Twig stepped in, but Mr. Murley caught her arm.

Inside the cabin, a girl a few years younger than Twig sat on a long vinyl bench. She scooted over meaningfully.

"This is Casey. She's so excited to meet you. You'll be rooming together."

Mr. Murley looked at Casey in an expectant but gentle way. Casey emitted a meek, "Hi."

"Casey's been with us a few weeks now."

That was all Mr. Murley said about that, but Twig understood. *She's coming along. Soon she'll be shaking hands and smiling like the Daffodil Princess in the Puyallup parade. Soon you will too, Twig.*

No, Mr. Murley, Twig could've said if she were inclined to speak her mind these days. *I won't. That haunted island will swallow me up first. It wants to swallow all of you too.*

Casey's eyes were big and brown and sad. She looked clean, but she smelled like pony poo. Island Ranch was a pony farm—every little girl's dream.

Mr. Murley started up the engine. Casey looked out the window at the parking lot and dutifully returned Keely's wave, but Twig didn't bother. Casey wiggled closer to her, and Twig wanted to shrink back, but her backpack was in the way.

"I'm eight," Casey whispered. When Twig didn't comment, she said reverently, "Mrs. Murley said you're twelve." Casey was quiet for a minute. Then, "We each get our own pony. Did you know that?"

She paused again, waiting for Twig to respond.

"They're all Welsh ponies," Casey continued slowly, bravely. "I think they're prettier than Shetlands. My pony's name is Bedtime Story, but I call her Story. I know how to take care of her all on my own now. You'll have Rain Cloud."

How fitting. Through the rain-streaked window, Twig glanced at the island again, or tried to. It was wrapping its mist around the boat, tighter and tighter. The island was nothing but a blur of thicker mist with a few black gaps in between.

Mr. Murley said, "Don't worry about this weather, Twig. *Blue Molly* here can handle it just fine." She must not have looked very convinced, for he added, "It looks worse than it is."

Sometimes Keely took Twig and her stepsister, Emily, and stepbrother, Corey, to Steilacoom to walk along the beach and watch the ferry going back and forth to McNeil Island—the prison island. It was the first thing that had come out of Emily's mouth when Keely had told her and Corey about sending Twig to Island Ranch—"Like McNeil Island?"

Emily had been horrified. Even Emily, who was so sure Twig was guilty, didn't think Twig deserved to be imprisoned on an island. Keely had been quick to point out the ridiculousness of comparing a maximum-security prison facility to the pretty little pony farm.

Keely hadn't mentioned the ghosts. No one had.

The Murleys had just moved to the island and opened

their ranch for troubled girls a couple of months ago, though it had been under construction for several years. They'd been foster parents for forever. They were certified counselors, and the ranch was a registered private school. They had all the right credentials, Keely had assured Twig.

Twig didn't care whether the Murleys were capable of fixing her. She was plenty worried about how they'd try to do it, but she was more worried about the stories she'd found online. Had the Murleys heard those stories? Stories about the island, that had made Twig shudder, even in a stuffy, overheated apartment?

CHAPTER 3

LONEHORN ISLAND'S JAGGED SHORE reached for *Blue Molly*. Mr. Murley slowed the little boat down, and Twig cringed in anticipation of a rough meeting with the menacing black rock, but Mr. Murley began a wide turn. They skirted a point of cliffside, and there, sheltered on both ends by jutting rock formations about thirty feet high, was a sandy cove.

"Here we are—the lee of the island, our shelter in the storm."

Fine sand and a sturdy dock built onto the beach quieted Twig's fears, at least about never making it ashore. But the freshly built dock reminded her that this island wasn't accustomed to human inhabitants—at least not living ones.

Mr. Murley secured the boat and helped the girls out, then heaved out the suitcase.

A neat little boardwalk made its way from the dock to one side of the cove, along its edge, where soft sand met hard rock. Casey picked her way up the beach in a careful, wary way.

In front of her, Mr. Murley navigated the path with the suitcase. "It's a bit of a climb," he said between labored breaths. "We've got a freight dock on the other end of the island, where it's flatter, and an access road. But this beach is much closer, a straight shot to Cedar Harbor, so I keep *Blue Molly* docked here." He looked over his shoulder with a grin. "If I'd known about this," he said, nodding at the suitcase, "I would've left the truck on the other side and taken *Blue Molly* the long way around. I'll bet we could fit you *and* Casey in here."

Twig almost smiled. The suitcase was ridiculous, and poor Mr. Murley had to lug it she had no idea how far. She glanced ahead, at the top of the rocky incline above the beach. Small red-barked trees with twisting branches clung to the rocks. But beyond them was the evergreen wood. The path would take them into the thick of that wood, into the misty, shadowy heart of the island.

Behind Twig was the crushing of the waves. Beyond

the water was Keely, waiting to go home, to the home that could never be one for Twig. A past with ghosts she knew all too well, that were all too real. Ahead was Island Ranch, whose ghosts were rumor and wisp. Maybe she'd dare to hope that they weren't real, that this really could be a beginning.

"The truck's just up this way," Mr. Murley said. "It's not far."

They'd reached the top of the rocks, overlooking the beach. Mr. Murley's smile was warm, but he glanced at the trees with a trace of uneasiness. He held out a strong hand for Casey and she took it. Twig quickened her step.

Casey stopped suddenly and pointed to the sky. "Mr. Murley! Your bird!"

Mr. Murley let go of the suitcase handle and fumbled in his pocket. Twig searched the sky but saw only drizzle.

Mr. Murley aimed his phone upward, then jerked it toward the trees. "Got it! I think this is my best one yet."

He showed the picture to the girls. It was little more than a bright green blur of wings, disappearing into the darker evergreens, but Casey said, "Oh! Taylor's gonna like that one."

"We have a mystery bird here on the island," Mr. Murley explained. "It's become a hobby of mine, trying to spot it. And I seem to have sucked one of our girls, Taylor, into it too. She's determined to identify it for me."

The boardwalk gave way to a gravel path that wound through thickening woods. Just a couple of turns along that path, and the only reminders of the openness of the water were the mist and the lichen floating from the branches like ghost hair.

Something shifted in the trees, a shadow within the shadows.

A deer? No, Twig knew the movement of a deer. At the old house in McKenna, whenever Mom's friends came over, Twig would skid down the ravine beyond the broken-down cars, away from the laughter that grated her ears. The river's reassuring song, washing everything else away, would sometimes be interrupted by the soft-snap footsteps of a fawn and doe. They'd look at her with their big brown eyes like Casey's, then go on working their way through the riverbed, accepting Twig as part of the woods.

The island's woods were different—denser, darker, deeper, powerful, and alone. Black-green evergreens wrapping themselves in shadow. And this movement was different too. Careful like a deer, but much bigger and paler—ghost-white.

Twig realized she'd stopped walking, that Mr. Murley and Casey were slipping out of view. Mr. Murley must not have noticed her absence, with the grinding and thunking of the bulky suitcase on the mud and gravel path.

There was a distinctive thump from the woods just behind Twig, and she froze.

A large white animal was barely visible through the tangle of early spring bramble, through the softening and shifting haze of the morning mist. A horse. The thump must have been its rider dismounting. It had to be Mrs. Murley or one of the other girls. But the chill creeping along Twig's spine, under her shell, told her otherwise.

Part hidden by the wood, part blurred by mist, the human figure stepped forward. The mist shifted and a ghostly pair of pale brown eyes locked with Twig's. Fearless, determined, searching eyes. Just the eyes and a messy pile of light brown hair were visible. A ghost boy.

CHAPTER 4

THE GHOST BOY SLIPPED back into the trees. He moved like something that was used to being unseen, that was hidden as a manner of being, and not out of fear.

"Twig?" Mr. Murley called. "Are you okay?"

Mr. Murley was coming back for her, with Casey and the suitcase in tow.

Twig's eyes flicked at the woods again. A flurry of movement, then nothing. She ran to Mr. Murley's side. Mr. Murley looked down at her, concerned. Feeling silly for running to him, Twig pulled back. Casey caught her eye. She looked at the woods and then back at Twig. She squeezed her eyes shut and leaned harder into Mr. Murley's side.

"Well," Mr. Murley said, "good thing I didn't lose you already. Mrs. Murley would never let me hear the end of it."

Twig hurried ahead, not quite running. The path widened to a gravel circle. A truck was parked there, pointed toward a dirt road. Twig hurried straight to it and climbed in, scooting over for Casey.

The boy's eyes kept glaring at her in her mind, unflinching, no matter how she tried to blink them away. He was one of the island's ghosts; he had to be. But that was stupid. There were no such things as ghosts. Mom believed in ghosts, but Mom was *Mom*.

"Glad you're anxious to see your new home," Mr. Murley said as he entered the truck.

Anxious was an understatement. Right now Twig didn't care if it really was a prison; she wanted some walls between her and these woods and the ghost boy and his horse. A ghost horse. Just like the stories.

•••

When they reached the end of the road, the sky opened up over a clearing and Twig could see the house in front of them, just like the pictures on the website—a big rambler painted a yellow whose sunniness could hardly be dampened by the drizzle. A white porch wrapped around the building. On one side of the house was a carport and a tractor shed, and on the other was a barn-red stable. Beyond the buildings lay the pastures—six acres of pasture, according to Island Ranch's website—all enclosed and divided into sections with split-rail fences.

The ranch looked welcoming, so long as Twig didn't glance at the forest that hunched over it, dark and hungry.

As they pulled up to a gate at the driveway entrance, a girl about nine years old came running out of the stable. Her hood flapped and her boots stomped. She waved and opened the gate.

The pony pastures were already fenced in, so what was the gate for? Maybe to keep the ghost riders out. Twig shivered, then assured herself it must be to keep out deer. She followed Casey out of the truck, and the other girl met them in the driveway.

Mr. Murley hefted her suitcase from the truck bed. "Twig, this is Janessa."

"Hi." Janessa smiled and extended a hand.

"Hi." Something about Janessa caught Twig off guard and made her forget, until the word slipped out, that she had plans to say absolutely nothing. She remembered just in time to keep her hands stuffed in her jacket pockets.

Beyond the carport, the clouds shifted and a thin ray of sunlight peeked through. It felt different in the yard, with the gate shut securely, though it was silly to think a gate could shut out ghosts, could shut out the wild determination of the island. But even Mr. Murley seemed to truly relax now that they were home.

Home. Even without the hauntedness of the island, could this cheery yellow house, in its peaceful bubble of fenced-in pasture, really be home for someone like Twig?

Twig inched out of the shelter of the carport. The yard smelled like ponies, like they'd always been here, but the buildings still smelled of fresh paint.

Janessa ran ahead to the front door, dark brown frizz springing out of her braids with every bounce. Casey looked up at Twig uncertainly, as though she weren't quite sure what to do with her, but she stuck close by Twig's side. The fear of the woods had left Casey's eyes, and a rush of relief filled them, convincing Twig that she knew something about Ghost Boy.

Janessa threw the front door open, and the aroma of

pancakes and bacon ushered them in, causing Twig's stomach to do a new flop that was more hunger and happiness than anxiety. She stiffened her shoulders back up and told herself she'd better not let herself relax so easily. Who knew what these people were really like?

CHAPTER 5

THE FRONT DOOR OPENED to a spacious entryway. A strip of indoor-outdoor carpet stretched to a row of shelves and coat hooks over wooden benches.

Mr. Murley held out his hand to Twig—for her jacket. Twig blinked at him, hesitating, then made her decision. She shrugged off her shell as if it were nothing, as if it hadn't kept everything that threatened to fall apart inside of her together where it belonged this morning. She let Mr. Murley take it and hang it up, but she kept her mini-backpack on. She removed her shoes, then the soppy socks. The floor was nice and warm. Everything was warm. Stupid as she knew it was, she wanted to forget about Ghost Boy, to forget about Keely, to forget about Daddy and everything else, and she wanted to like it here.

When Twig looked up, a small woman with fluffy,

shoulder-length dark hair was standing in front of her, pulling the sleeves of her sweater down from where they'd been pushed up around her elbows.

"I'm Mrs. Murley." She didn't try to shake hands; she went straight for the hug—quick but warm and soft. "We built this home for six girls, and now that you're here, Twig, it's complete. Welcome home, honey." Twig made herself pull away, but Mrs. Murley pretended not to notice. "Girls!" she said. "Twig is here!"

Two girls ran into the entryway, and another lagged nonchalantly behind.

Taylor, Mandy, and Regina each introduced themselves, each offered her a hand to shake, and each gave her a knowing look when she didn't return the gesture. Mandy's smile looked more like a scowl, but the rest of them seemed okay.

"You're the oldest now." Regina tossed her heavy ponytail over her shoulder. Her dark eyes narrowed as she looked Twig up and down. But apparently the Murleys had already drilled enough manners into her to prevent her saying what she was thinking—*You sure don't look it.*

"You're just in time for breakfast," Mrs. Murley said.

Janessa smiled a great big smile. "On Saturdays we eat late, but we eat big."

"You ladies go ahead and get started," Mr. Murley said. "I had a bite before I left." And he wheeled Keely's suitcase down the hall.

Twig followed the others through a big room with floor-to-ceiling windows on one side and a massive stone fireplace on another, into an open dining and kitchen area.

Casey stayed right at Twig's elbow until the other girls all began pulling out chairs and sitting at the table. Then she pulled one out and stepped aside. "Here's your seat, Twig."

A great big mug was set there, its contents completely hidden by the pile of whipped cream oozing over the rim. Steam curled up from it like crooked fingers, beckoning Twig with rich, chocolaty promises.

"Thanks."

Twig scooched her chair in and sat 'on her knees in order to be taller. The table was heaped with platters of pancakes and ham and bacon and potatoes. Sliced strawberries. Orange juice and milk. But no one was eating. Twig stopped with her hand halfway to her fork. What were they waiting for?

"Is it my turn?" Mandy's short blond curls sprang out with an exuberance that defied her saggy posture and her droopy eyes.

"No," the girl called Taylor said, "it's mine."

Mandy grabbed one of Twig's hands, Casey the other. Twig cringed. She slipped free of Mandy's grasp, and Mandy didn't fight it. But Twig peeked at Casey out of the corner of her eye—Casey, who was squeezing her hand tighter. Twig let her hold it.

Taylor bowed her tightly braided head. Her prayer was short and serious. When she said, "Amen," Twig grabbed her fork and stabbed the biggest pancake on the platter. She hadn't had pancakes in ages.

Janessa seemed to be the talker of the group. She babbled on about the girls' ages and their ponies and what they were studying in school and whose chores were whose. Twig didn't pay much attention. There was some kind of thick apple cider syrup that kept begging her to pour more on; it was just about the best thing she'd ever tasted besides the hot chocolate, and she was busy cramming cider-soaked pancake into her mouth and wondering what someone so disgustingly cheerful as Janessa was doing here, on Lonehorn Island.

Twig raised her head to take a swig of hot chocolate, and Janessa locked eyes with her. "I'm a thief," she blurted, as though she'd read Twig's mind.

"Ja*nessa.*" Taylor frowned. "Do you always have to do that?"

"Oh," Twig said. Not reading her mind then. She swallowed a thick, chocolaty mouthful. "Thanks for the heads-up." She had plans to sleep with her mini-backpack under her pillow anyway. The rest of her stuff, she didn't care about. Except the jacket. She liked that jacket now. But she didn't see how Janessa could get any use out of that without getting caught.

"That's in the past now," Mrs. Murley said without a blink.

"Janessa has to tell everybody new who comes what she did." Regina rolled her eyes.

Janessa shrugged. "Everybody has to tell, eventually."

Janessa's eyes flicked to Twig. Twig had never said it, what she'd done. Would saying it over and over again make it shrink somehow? Maybe that was why Janessa did it. Or maybe it was just to challenge each new girl. Twig took another bite of pancake, chewed thoughtfully, and swallowed.

"I almost killed my stepsister," Twig said. "Could I have

some more hot chocolate, please?" There. Now nobody had a chance to try to get her to tell.

Regina snorted. "Is that supposed to scare us?"

Twig shrugged. She supposed it should've scared them if it were true.

"Regina," Mrs. Murley said sternly.

"Sorry."

"Here." Casey passed Twig a big white pitcher. "Hot chocolate."

Mr. Murley joined them at the table. "Second breakfast," he said cheerfully. "I must be turning into a hobbit."

A couple of the girls giggled, but Twig didn't get the joke. She poured her hot chocolate, and the girls passed food and talked about ponies, like everything was normal. Like Twig was normal. Well, none of them were normal, or they wouldn't be here. And the Murleys weren't normal either, or they wouldn't be giving all these messed-up girls ponies to ride and hot chocolate with whipped cream and sprinkles.

On a haunted island.

"We're the only ones here?" Twig aimed her question at Mrs. Murley. "On the island?"

To Twig's horror, the other girls stopped talking. Mrs. Murley smiled, and Twig knew that Keely had told them about the not talking thing. This was more than just a quick thanks or a snippy remark or a request for more food. It was an honest-to-goodness question, the kind that threatened to start an actual conversation.

"Just us girls and Mr. Murley."

"No boys?"

Mr. Murley raised his eyebrows over his mug of coffee. Janessa giggled. Regina let out a sulky breath and rolled her dark eyes. She was a year younger than Twig, but Twig could tell she wanted to be older.

"No boys," she said miserably.

"Except for the wild boy," Casey said, barely above a breath.

So Casey had seen Ghost Boy, only she called him *the wild boy*. Twig recalled the wild, searching eyes. *Wild* seemed to suit him just as well.

Regina mumbled something about wishing there really were a wild boy, but Mrs. Murley said, "Casey, hon, we've talked about that."

"I'm not telling stories," Casey said.

"I like her stories," Regina remarked.

Mrs. Murley smiled again. "So long as everyone understands that they're stories."

Casey shut up, but she looked at Twig knowingly. Her eyes said, *You know he's real. You've seen him too.*

CHAPTER 6

AFTER THEY'D CLEARED THE table, Twig followed Casey to their bedroom. The far half of the wall, nearest the window, was bare, while the near side was plastered with crayon drawings and drippy watercolor paintings, mostly of horselike blobs. Casey's side of the room. Casey's comforter was hot pink. A baby doll's scratched plastic head and arms peeked out from under the taut bedding. The doll's head rested on a generous pink pillow, eyelids shut.

Twig's bed was draped in pale green, crowned with a plump, plain blue pillow. Her favorite colors. But the massive, dark gray suitcase stood upright at the foot of the bed like a tombstone. The heavy suitcase had even dug itself into the green comforter. She shoved the suitcase over, onto its side. There, that was better.

She was glad she didn't have time to unpack. They had to get to the stable. The ponies were waiting, Casey said. Twig did have to open the suitcase to get out the big shoe box, though, the one that held the boots Keely had bought at a western store, according to the Murleys' recommendation. They were plain black leather, with tapered toes.

Twig struggled to work her feet into them, then wobbled to a stand. "Just a little heel," Keely had said, but a little bit was too much for feet that were used to the worn-through soles of cheap canvas slides.

"They make you look taller," Casey said consolingly. "The heels and the pointy toes are for your stirrups."

The soles were hard and slick and felt weird. Twig didn't like having her feet in shoes that weren't her shoes.

"They'll feel better once they're broken in," Casey said.

Mrs. Murley was waiting on the porch. All six girls skipped past her, down the steps, and into the yard.

"All set, Twig?"

Twig shifted her mini-backpack under her shell and nodded to Mrs. Murley. Though thin rays of sunlight filtered through the front windows and a soft breeze was dusting the last of the mist away, she zipped up her shell.

"You've missed the early morning chores, but the mid-morning chores are the fun part." Mrs. Murley winked at the other girls.

"We got up at six to feed them." Casey tucked a lock of straight brown hair behind her ear. "Now it's time to clean out the stalls, then exercise them."

At the stable, Twig could hear the ponies nickering their anticipation through the door. Taylor and Janessa thrust the stable doors open. They called out to their ponies as if they were old friends. The wide doors opened to a wider aisle. On either side, pony heads reached over stall doors, ears perked up. The ears pivoted toward Twig; the eyes followed her too. As she passed by, each pony made a noisy breath that seemed to be directed right at her. Twig made sure she stayed in the middle, where they couldn't reach her.

Sunlight shone through a row of skylights above the neatly swept aisle. The stall doors were painted grass green and a plaque hung on each one. Bright letters, some brushed on with wobbly hands, spelled out the name of each pony. Twig followed Mrs. Murley past the stalls of Sparkler, Chatterbox, Gadget, Celeste, and Bedtime Story—to another stall, like the others, but without a plaque.

Mrs. Murley smiled at Twig expectantly. From the stall came a loud sniffling in, then a snuffle out, right in Twig's face. Twig squinted against it. When she opened her eyes, she was looking right into the big, glaring, dark eye of a pony. His gray ears flicked toward her and away, toward her and away, then settled, cupped toward her. He lowered his head and his lip curled up. Twig shrank back, expecting a snarl, even a nip, but the pony just lipped the edge of his stall door.

"You'll make Rain Cloud's nameplate," Mrs. Murley said, "once you're sure you want to be his rider—once you think he's sure about you too."

This creature, pulling its head back to scrutinize her, was supposed to be her pony? Well, he was no dumb pony, Twig had to give him that. Unfortunately, that probably meant he was smart enough to dislike Twig.

"Hi there, Rain Cloud. I've got somebody new here for you to meet. Just hold your hand out now, Twig, like this."

Twig held her hand out, palm down, fingers curled, like Mrs. Murley's, but she scrunched her eyes shut, certain that this animal was not going to want her bony hand intruding in its personal space.

"Now, you want to move slow and easy, like this, so you

don't startle him. When you're calm, he's calm. Nice and easy. Don't worry, Twig, it's not you. He just senses that you're new to this, is all. The more comfortable you get, the more he'll trust you."

Twig moved a hand tentatively toward the pony again, then jerked it back when Rain Cloud rotated his ears abruptly toward her and glared through the long, black strands of his mane.

"Try talking to him calmly just like I am."

Twig shook her head. She couldn't talk to anyone like Mrs. Murley did. Especially not a pony who was laughing at her with his haughty eyes and his snorty breath. Especially not in front of the other girls.

So Mrs. Murley let Twig stand aside and watch as she and the girls turned out Mrs. Murley's tawny horse, Feather, along with the ponies into one of the pastures.

"Well, Twig." Mrs. Murley put an arm around her shoulders and gave her a quick squeeze. "I'll leave you to clean out the stalls. I've got some papers to correct in the house. Casey'll show you the ropes."

Twig's stomach did a little flop. Did that mean what she thought it meant?

Mrs. Murley left, and Twig went back into the stable with the others. The girls began picking up funny-looking rakes, plucking piles of pony poo and soaking-wet wood shavings, and depositing them in buckets. And Mrs. Murley expected her to do it too. Today. Right now.

CHAPTER 7

"COME ON, TWIG," CASEY said. "We'll do it together. First, Story's stall and then Rain Cloud's." She offered Twig a rake. Twig just stared at it, but Casey nudged it at her insistently, her dark, delicate brows furrowed.

Twig took it. Well, if Mrs. Murley was leaving, she couldn't leave little Casey to do double the work. And she supposed it was only right that she do something to earn that breakfast.

The stable doors were left open to let the fresh, cool air in. Still, it was hard, smelly work, and Twig had to stop to unzip her shell.

After they'd cleaned out both stalls, they dumped the buckets of soiled bedding into a wheelbarrow. Casey grabbed the handles of the wheelbarrow and jerked at it, trying in vain to tip it up onto its wheel.

"I guess we should've dumped one stall at a time," Casey said breathlessly.

Casey struggled with the wheelbarrow. She was sturdy for her size, but she was getting nowhere. Twig examined her own skinny fingers. She wasn't made for this kind of thing. She glanced around the stable. Everyone else was outside. Twig had no desire to shovel that manure back out of the wheelbarrow in order to lighten it, and nobody else was going to push it.

"Oh, here," Twig said. "Just give it to me. I'll do it."

Casey relinquished the handles and blew her bangs out of her eyes with a breath of relief. "Thanks," she said sheepishly.

Twig grimaced and put her whole body weight, little though there was, into it. The wheelbarrow teetered sideways, then, mercifully, onto its wheel. She ran with it before it had a chance to change its mind and tip back down. Who would've thought two little ponies could produce such a load in just one day? She couldn't wait to see the size of the muck heap.

She found the rut worn through the grass by repeated wheelbarrowing and struggled over the bumpy, wet earth toward the edge of the clearing. Had Twig known beforehand what a long a way it was to the muck heap, she might not have offered to push after all.

"So we don't smell the stink all the time!" Casey shouted over her shoulder as she ran ahead of Twig and the wheelbarrow, showing her the way.

But that meant, of course, that they had to smell it all the way there. Her arms shook, and she pushed harder with her legs. The last thing she wanted was to let the wheelbarrow back down and fight with it in front of Regina, who was sauntering back to the stable with an empty wheelbarrow.

After she finally got to dump it out, Twig gave the wheelbarrow a look of disgust and turned her back on it. Casey could bring it back now.

Mrs. Murley emerged from the stable. When she smiled at Twig and Casey, her dark eyes glittered. "Looks good in there, girls. A good student and a good teacher."

Casey blushed and ducked to hide her smile. Twig zipped her shell back up.

• • •

After lunch, some of the girls went back out to ride their ponies. They'd met all their behavior goals for the week, and Mrs. Murley was going to take them on a ride down to the beach, now that the sun was out and the mist was gone. The others pouted and then resigned themselves to sprawling in the living room with a game of Monopoly. There didn't seem to be any TV at Island Ranch. Well, Twig was used to no TV, from back when she was with Mom. They hadn't even had power in their house. Not that it was really their house, as the police had made plain when they came to clear the squatters out— and found the other stuff Mom was doing. And found Twig.

Mr. Murley suggested that now would be a good time for Casey to help Twig unpack, so Twig followed her back to their room and they both sat on the bed and stared at the suitcase.

Twig made no move to unpack, and Casey got more and more wiggly and uneasy, until she finally said, "Well, at least get out your pajamas, then, if you're just going to leave tomorrow."

Twig took out some sweats to sleep in and shoved the suitcase onto the floor and crossed her arms. Casey bit her lip and left.

She couldn't go back to Keely. But how could she stay here and feel useless and stupid and have a pony just to remind her of that, day after day? Maybe she'd be better off sneaking into the forest and letting the island's ghosts destroy her first. What would saying something like that do for her behavior goals?

Twig opened up her backpack and took out several folded-up sheets of paper and flattened them on the bed. She'd printed out these stories she'd found online about Lonehorn Island. The abandoned island. The island that early pioneers had disappeared from, that others had fled, claiming ghostly horses and phantom riders had driven them out. In the 1990s, a family had tried to camp on the island. They'd come back with stories of ghost horses and riders, and strange, deadly, flashing blades.

Some said the riders were armed with these weapons; some said it was the horses. Some said the ghosts were Edward Murley, who bought the whole island for a steal in the 1890s, and his three sons, who'd died, along with their ponies, in mysterious riding accidents, one after the other, before the family finally gave up on the island. They were the ones who'd named it, the ones who'd passed it down from generation to generation, to the current owner, Mr. David Murley.

Twig didn't come out until dinner, and no one tried to make her. Dinner was pot roast dripping with gravy, and potatoes and carrots that had simmered in the Crock-Pot all day. At Mom's, she'd gotten by on canned tuna and dry cornflakes and plain white bread. Keely fed her pasta drizzled with olive oil, accompanied by a few skimpy strips of grilled chicken.

When the beef was all gone, Twig resorted to sneaking finger-swipes of gravy from her plate. Mr. Murley winked at her, passed her the basket of dinner rolls, and showed her how to use them to sop the gravy up.

After dinner, it was back to the ponies. The mist had returned, a light fog that watered down the setting sun. Twig followed the girls to the pasture and stood there with her hands in her jacket pockets, watching their ponies come to them and nuzzle them.

In the woods behind the pasture shelter, Twig caught a glimpse of movement. She ran over to the fence and peered into the trees, just in time to see the back of someone disappear swiftly, quietly, into the brush. Ghost Boy! Twig held her breath. She stood still and she looked and looked, but he was gone. No horse this time, as far as she could tell. Maybe he was trying to be more careful. But careful of what? What did a ghost have to be careful of?

Regina walked by with her pony's lead in hand and caught Twig frowning at the trees.

"I like it here," Regina admitted with a shrug, "but those woods give me the creeps. Like there's something out there. I'd stick to the clearing if I were you."

Twig nodded vaguely. She didn't think Regina had seen Ghost Boy. Maybe she was like Mr. Murley—just had a feeling something wasn't quite right.

"There's some nice paths where we ride." Regina pointed across the pasture. "That way, there's a little meadow. Mr. Murley was planning on clearing more trails through the woods, but now, I don't know."

Twig looked at her questioningly.

"He keeps finding some reason to put it off." Regina ran her fingers absently through her pony's mane. "Your mom's coming tomorrow?"

"Stepmom."

"Are you going back with her?"

Twig shrugged. Could she really do this every day? How long would it be before they expected her to do it all herself, like the other girls? How long would it be before Rain Cloud made his dislike for her painfully clear?

●●●

Mrs. Murley approached Twig. Casey had gone into the stable without her, without offering to help. She hadn't said a word to Twig since the suitcase.

"Why don't you try to catch him this time?"

Rain Cloud was the last pony left in the pasture. Twig shook her head, so Mrs. Murley called Rain Cloud. She rubbed his forehead and clipped on his lead rope. Then she handed it to Twig. Reluctantly, Twig pulled her hands out of her jacket pockets and took hold of the lead. She stepped toward the stable. Rain Cloud followed, keeping a scornful eye on Twig. Twig was certain the pony was dragging his feet just a little, but Mrs. Murley didn't seem to notice.

Twig got Rain Cloud settled with fresh water and feed, then slid past him, out of the stall. She shut the door with a sigh of relief. She'd survived her first stint at pony managing.

Casey was just finishing up with Story. Twig offered her a small, apologetic smile, and Casey plunked a brush back into Story's grooming kit and smiled back weakly.

Twig leaned her back against Rain Cloud's door and noticed something she hadn't seen before at the end of the row. There was the stall for Mrs. Murley's horse, Feather, much bigger than the ponies' stalls, and right next to it, another large stall with a plaque engraved by a grown-up hand that read "Caper."

There was no head peeking over this stall, no nickering from the other side of the door. And while Feather had been a part of the chore routine just like the ponies, Twig had yet to see another horse or to hear any mention of the name *Caper*.

Across the walkway, Taylor gave her pony a last rub on the nose and latched her stall door. "That was Mr. Murley's horse," she said, even more seriously than usual.

"Was?"

"He died. Something…got him. That's why Mr. Murley rebuilt the fence. That's why it's so high."

Casey whispered in Twig's ear, "The wild horses ate him."

Prickles ran down the back of Twig's neck. Something

shifted behind her, grabbed her by the ear. She shrieked, pulled back, and banged her head against the stall wall. She turned around to face the ghost horse, the wild creature, whatever it was that was trying to eat her.

Twig found herself looking right into one of Rain Cloud's dark, skeptical eyes.

"It's just Rain Cloud," Taylor said with the slightest hint of a smile.

Regina erupted in laughter.

"Trying to taste you." Casey patted Twig's hand. "He just wants to get to know you." Then, in the lowest of whispers, "He's a good pony. Not like those things in the woods."

CHAPTER 8

TWIG SHOVED HER STILL-PACKED suitcase a little farther toward the foot of her bed. She peeled the green comforter back. The sheets were cool, and she was tired.

Casey's doll fell to the floor, and one fake eye rattled open, the other shut. Twig picked it up so that Casey wouldn't have to reach down for it. You never knew what was under the bed, especially when you were only eight. Twig tucked it next to Casey.

"Thanks."

"Welcome." Twig turned back to her own bed, then hesitated. "I saw him again."

"The wild boy?"

Twig sat on the edge of her bed and folded her arms across her chest. "Do you know who he is?"

Casey shook her head. "He's been here all along, I think. But I never seen him until a couple days ago. I think he's looking for something."

Casey didn't seem to know about the ghost stories, didn't seem to think the boy was a ghost. Twig decided it was best not to mention that possibility just yet. "I wonder what he could be looking for," Twig said, then, more to herself, "and why's he looking here?"

When Casey didn't answer, Twig curled up on the top half of her bed and pulled the comforter up over her shoulders.

"Mr. Murley has a gun," Casey whispered into the silence. "Just in case. Regina told me. He keeps it locked up somewhere."

"Hmm," Twig said. Somehow she didn't think Ghost Boy would care one whit about Mr. Murley's gun.

• • •

Twig gave up trying to get to sleep. She grabbed her mini-backpack from under her pillow, just in case, and crept out of bed and into the hall. A nightlight glowed reassuringly, showing the way to the front of the house. Though the wall of windows on the pasture side of the house revealed only a thick, low fog, moonlight streamed into the living room through the skylights in the sloping roof—a paler, wilder sort of light that gave her a chill.

Someone had left the kitchen light on. She headed for the lit-up kitchen, away from the searching island moon, and she paused in front of the refrigerator. Printed on photo paper and magneted to the fridge was the blurry, green picture Mr. Murley had taken on their way up from the cove. Someone, probably Taylor, had added the caption, "Mr. Murley's Bird, Lonehorn Island, Washington," followed by the date.

Beside it, under a magnet made of baked clay smooshed into the shape of a horse, was an index card, stained with a ring of coffee and bearing the neatly printed words "Let us not grow weary in doing good, for in due season we shall reap if we do not lose heart."

What a strange place she'd ended up in. But the food was good. Were midnight snacks allowed? Well, she'd find out soon enough. Pondering who was supposed to not lose heart—the Murleys or the girls—she pulled the door open, then jolted.

A high whinny broke the near silence of a kitchen at midnight, pierced the buzz of the ceiling light, the hum of the refrigerator. Twig's heart beat faster. She gripped the fridge handle tighter. It was nothing. She was going to have to get used to living here, to animal sounds.

Another whinny. Twig froze. This whinny was desperate; as little as Twig knew about horses, there was no denying that. A shiver ran down the back of her neck.

Twig shook the shiver off and slammed the refrigerator door shut. She'd lost her appetite. But even without the cold draft from the fridge, the shiver came back. This was silly. Why would any of the ponies be desperate? There was no one here to bother them. The stable doors were latched tight against wild animals. Ponies made noises. Maybe one of them was having a bad dream. Did ponies dream?

But no pony whinny from inside the stable could travel into the kitchen so clear like that. Was there a pony outside the stable?

Another whinny—more of a scream. Twig scrambled up onto the counter, reached over the sink, and tore the curtains back. The three-quarter moon hovered high above the tree line, but the low fog hung heavy in the yard, shifting slowly. In the fog, something else moved. It might have been invisible if it weren't moving in the opposite direction of the mist. Twig gasped. No ranch pony had made that whinny! It belonged to the ghostly form flowing against the mist.

CHAPTER 9

GHOST BOY AND HIS horse formed a gray-white silhouette, creeping through the shifting fog. Ghost Boy leaned toward another pale, phantomlike form. He was riding one horse and holding the lead of another, pulling it along. It followed, but not without tossing its head and kicking up the turf right beside the boy. Where was he going? Then Twig realized—he was headed right for the stable!

Twig half fell off the counter and skidded across the glossy hardwood floor, through the great room and the entryway, to the front door. She paused, fingers trembling on the deadbolt. What was she thinking, going out there? She'd just open the door, real quiet, and watch. At least she could know. She had to know. She slid the bolt and eased the door open, then slipped out into the shadows of the porch. She searched the fog for any movement that didn't belong to the mist, but the yard was empty. She was too late. Ghost Boy was gone.

No, not gone. The stable door was standing wide open. Inside, ponies neighed and snorted indignantly. There was a deeper, wilder snort and cry—a horse cry. Was Ghost Boy in there?

Twig was still frozen there, trying to decide what to do, when the boy emerged. His cloak billowed in the wind, moss green—or maybe it was mist blue. Moonlight filtered through the mist and skittered over it, shifting the color of the fabric. It wasn't just the moonlight, Twig realized; the cloak itself was a dapple of colors, like Daddy's camouflage.

Ghost Boy shut the stable doors carefully, silently. His horse made a low, warning whinny and pawed at the ground. The boy stiffened for a fraction of an instant, listening, or maybe sensing in some other way, just as the horse had, a presence in the night. Then the boy sprang into action with a heightened urgency. He slammed the latch in place, gave the doors a jerk to test them. Gone was all concern for stealth. He caught the horse's lead just as a fearsome animal noise came from far off in the woods—distinctly horselike, but just as distinctly predatory.

Twig had never heard a horse sound described as a howl, but *howl* was the only word for the noise coming from the woods. Then came a whole chorus of the same sounds. Twig yelped, and Ghost Boy jumped and looked right at her. His cloak flapped in the wind with a sharp snap, and he looked as though he wanted to say something just as sharp, but he leaped onto the horse's back instead.

Torn-up earth flew with the horse's every bounding step. The gate was open, but the boy and his horse jumped the fence instead, and they disappeared into the mist and the shadows, where, in the distance, wild things whinny-howled. The warmth and safety of the house beckoned Twig, begged her to lock herself in, away from the island's secrets—secrets that were no longer content to be left alone. Secrets that were also searching.

Twig wanted to run in and bolt the door, but the gate at the end of the driveway, the only entrance to the safe little bubble of house and stable and paddocks, was standing wide open. Ghost Boy must've opened it to bring the other horse in—the horse that was now unaccounted for. Twig squeezed her eyes shut, took a deep breath, and ran for the gate. The wind and the whinny-howls in her ears nearly drove her to scream.

The steel gate was cold and night-wet in her hands. She banged it shut and latched it. But as soon as she did, she realized how stupid that was. If Ghost Boy could jump the fence, who was to say that whatever was out there couldn't too?

And what if she hadn't shut it out at all? What if she'd just shut it *in*? What had happened to the other horse? Twig took a few steps toward the stable. The ponies were making quiet, unhappy noises—not desperate noises, but still, something wasn't right. Something was different. Did she dare find out what?

CHAPTER 10

"TWIG?" A VOICE CALLED into the night.

Twig jolted and spun around. Mrs. Murley's silhouette was framed in the doorway. Twig didn't know whether to feel relieved or to wish Mrs. Murley would go away. She'd never know now if she had the guts to go into that stable.

"What is it?"

Twig glanced at the stable, then back at Mrs. Murley.

"I don't suppose you're planning on running away, barefoot and in your pajamas?"

Running away? Twig's mini-backpack rubbed against her hips. Oh. She shook her head.

"Well, your stepmom will be here tomorrow if you want to talk about going home."

Twig just shook her head again. Her head was full of

half-formed sentences, attempts to say something, to do something about what she'd just seen. *Mrs. Murley, there was a ghost boy in the yard. Mrs. Murley, I think there might be a ghost horse in the stable. Mrs. Murley, you need a higher fence. Mrs. Murley, didn't you hear those cries in the woods? There's something out there—a pack of them, a herd.* And rattling around those thoughts was the name *Caper,* along with Casey's words, *The wild horses ate him,* and *He's a good pony, not like those things in the woods.*

The ponies were just innocent animals, and the girls loved them. Twig shook her head again, this time at herself.

"Well, then, why don't you come back in, and I'll make you some tea. Or," Mrs. Murley said with a new spark of hope and enthusiasm, "hot chocolate?"

So she'd noticed how much Twig had liked that particular part of breakfast.

Twig let out one last shudder as Mrs. Murley bolted the door behind them.

"Don't even know why we lock it," Mrs. Murley said absently. "Just a habit I guess. There's no one else on this island."

"You should lock it," Twig said firmly.

Mrs. Murley let out a little, "Oh." But then she

smiled. "There are some throw blankets on the couch. Why don't you grab one and come in the kitchen and I'll make that chocolate?"

•••

When Twig's eyes flashed open, someone was leaning over her. Ghost Boy? He wanted to feed her to the forest. Twig shoved at him. There was a thump and a little yelp.

A little, girlish yelp.

Twig blinked the dream out of her head. Casey's big brown eyes stared up at her from the floor. Twig had knocked her off the bed.

But Casey bounced right up. "Sorry. I didn't mean to scare you, but you wouldn't wake up. Come on. We have to go feed the ponies."

Twig was too tired to move, certainly too tired to care about keeping Rain Cloud waiting for his breakfast. She'd been up late listening to Mrs. Murley talk about her first pony when she was a girl, and drinking hot chocolate and nodding.

Mrs. Murley hadn't expected Twig to say anything back. Not like her teachers. She'd stopped talking to them when Daddy got deployed. She'd gotten so full of stuff on the inside that she made herself blank on the outside. She'd written "Twig" on the top of her papers and she'd left the rest blank—clean, white spaces; fresh blue lines.

When the hot chocolate was gone, Twig had lain in bed, drifting in and out of sleep, jolting awake as soon as she nodded off, convinced she'd heard more of that strange horse-howling in the woods.

Twig sat on the edge of the bed, unmoving, while Casey pulled on jeans and a sweater. Twig had decided her pajama sweats would do. She could hear Mrs. Murley banging around in the kitchen. Getting their breakfast, she hoped. Was she tired too, after being up half the night?

Was Twig going to have to do this every morning? Were the hungry howls of ghost horses going to haunt her every night? Was Ghost Boy going to stare at her in her nightmares?

Keely would be here after breakfast. If Twig went with her, she could sleep in the car the whole way home. She could eat Keely's predictable Mediterranean diet dinners, get woken up by slamming apartment doors and honking horns, and be the same old blank paper Twig.

She stumbled after Casey and the other girls to the stable. By the time she got there, the doors were wide open and the ponies were nickering their morning greetings. Taylor came running back toward the door, her unzipped jacket flopping as she waved her arms.

"Oh!" Taylor gasped, her dark, serious eyes widening. "There's a horse. A real horse in there."

Twig was wide-awake now. *Run*, she wanted to scream. *It's a ghost horse*. But, remembering her cowardice the night before and not wanting to repeat it, she darted between the other girls, under Taylor's pointing arm, into the stable. What if it had devoured all the ponies and Feather? What if it had decided it liked it there and now it was going to haunt the stable forever?

She glanced from side to side as she ran, seeing only the curious faces of the ponies poking out of their stalls. Where was the horse?

As soon as she asked herself the question, Twig knew the answer: Caper's stall. That's where she'd have put it if she were Ghost Boy. Sure enough, the back of a white head was visible over Caper's door. Determined, Twig unlatched it. She took a breath, then flung it open. There was a wild neigh. Then the creature turned toward her, raised its head high, ears pinned back, and began to rear. The horse's coat was a glaring, surreal white, but the animal itself looked solid, absolutely real. If this creature kicked her, there would be no walking through the blow as if through the mist.

Twig almost screamed. Almost. But Casey was standing right next to her, mouth open, frozen. And she remembered what Mrs. Murley had said. She had to be calm. She had to be confident. Whether or not it was a ghost horse, it was still a horse of some kind, and she was the idiot who'd opened the stall door, who hadn't said a word to Mrs. Murley last night. Now it was up to her to keep them from getting trampled.

CHAPTER 11

EASY, GIRL," TWIG SAID soothingly. "Nice and easy."

The hooves lowered. The horse glared at her and pawed at the wood shavings. Its ears cupped forward, toward Twig.

"That's a good girl. Are you a girl? Are you a good girl?"

It was a stupid thing to say, but it was all Twig could come up with.

"That's it." The creature backed up a step. "That's a girl. Get the door, Casey, nice and slow."

Casey eased it shut. She slid the latch in place with a swift click.

"Keep talking to her, Twig," Janessa said. "I'll go get Mrs. Murley."

Twig didn't want to keep talking. She wanted to run out of that stable. But the solid wood of the stall door seemed to be enough to hold the animal back. The other girls whispered to each other behind her while she kept whispering nonsense. As she calmed the horse, Twig felt herself calming too. The other girls were transfixed, but not scared. If she could settle this thing like an ordinary horse, then maybe it *was* just an ordinary horse, not a ghost at all. Though the word *ordinary* hardly fit such an animal.

Aside from some mud spatters, its coat was dazzling white. It was smaller than Feather, but bigger than the ponies. Its build was strong but slender, all sleek and well-defined muscles—except for an oddly pronounced roundness to its belly.

Soft, pink skin showed through the white fuzz on its muzzle. Its mane was long and silky, almost shimmery. The ponies' manes were coarse as straw in comparison. Its forelock lay in a graceful curl above strange, gray eyes—flowing quicksilver eyes that regarded Twig, not with Rain Cloud's disdain, but with swirls of wild understanding and wilder fear.

Twig could've stared into those eyes forever, but Mrs. Murley's pounding feet just outside the stable, then her voice saying, "Janessa, you saw this horse?" brought her back to reality.

"Yes, Mrs. M, I saw it! It's not just one of Casey's stories. It's wild! It reared at us and—"

"Coming through, girls."

The girls parted, and Mrs. Murley's eyes moved from Twig, at the stall door, to the horse's magnificent head. "Oh my. How…"

Twig stepped aside, grateful to relinquish her horse-calming duty, to stand back and stare at the creature instead. She might be wild. She might even be dangerous. Twig wasn't sure exactly what she was, but she was certain she was no pony eater. She wasn't evil; she was magnificent.

"Hello, pretty lady," Mrs. Murley said in a quiet, awed voice. "How did you get here, girl?"

"Maybe she's a surprise from Mr. Murley," Regina said.

"Is it your birthday?" Janessa said.

Mrs. Murley shook her head and laughed anxiously. She held a hand out to the horse, and the horse sniffed it. "Stand back, girls, and be still. I'm going to have a closer look."

She undid the door and slipped into the stall with the mysterious horse.

"Well, Twig, she's good and calm now, isn't she? It

seems you're getting to know your way around horses quicker than anyone expected."

Casey smiled at Twig proudly, and Twig shrugged her shell up over her mouth.

"She's a true white. That's very rare. And she's unshod. Oh!" Mrs. Murley gasped. "But that's not possible!"

"What?" Mandy pushed past Taylor.

Casey peeked through the crack of the unlatched stall door. "Her hooves are weird."

Twig nudged the door open a bit more with her boot, though she kept her distance while she bent down. It was true. They looked more like a deer's than a horse's.

"Cloven hooves!" Mrs. Murley said.

Mrs. Murley composed herself and proceeded with her examination, but Twig could tell the hooves were bothering her—really bothering her.

"She can't be wild, not entirely. She's restless, but she's used to people. And she seems well cared for. But we're in for another extra horse."

Twig gulped. Did Mrs. Murley know about the other one? About Ghost Boy?

But Mrs. Murley said, "She's about to foal. Soon." She

straightened up and put her hands on her hips and took a step back to look the whole horse over. "Taylor," she said with a slight tremor in her voice, "go and get Mr. Murley, please. Quick, before he leaves for the boat."

Before he leaves to get Keely, Twig thought.

A moment later, Mr. Murley came in, panting, forehead crinkled in confusion, jogging after Taylor. He didn't say a word until Mrs. Murley had slipped out of the stall and opened the door so he could see.

"How did this happen? Even if there are wild horses on this island, how did one get in here?" His whisper was so low, Twig had to concentrate hard to hang on to it. "Maybe I should contact the sheriff."

"David," Mrs. Murley whispered back, "there's more to this mystery mare. Have a look at this." She pointed to the horse's feet.

"Some sort of crossbreed? Maybe we should get the vet to have a look."

"No!" Twig cried. The mystery mare was so beautiful, and she was left here all alone, and she was their secret. "She's not—she's not an ordinary horse. They'll think she's strange. They'll take her away and—"

"Run experiments or something!" Regina came to her side.

"Maybe she came to us for a reason," Taylor said.

"But if she's having a baby, and she's always been here on the island," Casey said, "that means—"

"There's another one." Mandy frowned. "Another something. It's creepy. I don't like it."

"You don't like anything!" Casey snapped.

"Girls!" Mr. Murley said in a stern, carefully low voice. The mystery horse had begun to lower her ears and snort in agitation. "Go and feed your ponies."

The other girls did as he said, but Twig lingered near Caper's stall for a moment.

There was another one. Her mate. It had to be Ghost Boy's horse—a stallion. Why would he just leave the mare? It was hard to imagine anyone not wanting her anymore, even a wild boy.

Yes, a wild boy. This horse was no ghost horse, and that meant Ghost Boy must not be a ghost after all. But still, the mystery mare was more than just an ordinary, tame horse, more even than a wild horse. So what did that make the boy? Was he something more than wild too?

A waft of warm breath breezed through Twig's tangled hair. Slowly, cautiously, she turned. Her pale blue eyes met the enormous, deep, silver eyes of the mystery mare. Something inside Twig felt like it was turning over. Mystery shook her forelock back and nickered faintly, a reserved sort of gratitude. Twig brought her hand up, slow, calm, and Mystery let her place it on her muzzle. Out of the corner of her eye, Twig saw Mrs. Murley open her mouth—to warn her that she was wild, that she might bite, Twig supposed—but Mr. Murley put a hand on Mrs. Murley's arm, and she said nothing.

"Mystery," Twig whispered. That was all, but she meant, *You're welcome*. And also, *Thank you*. And she knew that Mystery understood it.

"Well," Mr. Murley said quietly, "I'd better get going."

Keely! Twig didn't want her here, not even just to check on her; Keely didn't belong here. "Don't bring her here. Please. Tell her I want to stay."

"I'm glad you want to stay, Twig, but she's expecting—"

"I'll call her. I'll explain."

Mr. Murley was quiet for a minute. Then he said, "All right." He handed his cell phone to her.

She went outside, around the end of the stable. Under the shadows of its eaves, she dialed Keely's number.

"Hi."

"Twig?"

"Yeah. You don't need to come, okay?"

"But, Twig, I should—"

"It's okay. It doesn't matter. I need to stay here and I know it, and so you don't need to come."

"Well, I'll just come and see how you're doing and say good-bye."

"There's nothing to see, and we already said good-bye."

"You like it there?"

"I want to stay." Liking it here didn't have anything to do with anything. She wasn't going to ask Keely to take her back, and she wasn't going to leave before she found out who the wild boy was and what he was doing on this island. And she wasn't going to leave the mystery mare. Not yet.

CHAPTER 12

TWIG MADE HER EYES open. Someone was calling her name, someone much nicer than the people in her dream. She wanted to come out of it, but it was one of those heavy dreams that hung on her. The voice was just as insistent as the dream in its own way. It was a woman's voice, excited and soothing at the same time, saying, "Twig, Twig."

Mrs. Murley.

Twig opened her eyes again. This time they stayed open and they focused.

"Twig, do you want to see a miracle?"

Twig pushed herself up on her elbow and blinked into the night-lighted room. Was Mrs. Murley crazy? There were no such things as miracles.

"Our Mystery is foaling any minute. Hurry, or we'll miss it."

Twig pushed back her covers.

Mrs. Murley glanced at Casey, still curled up tight in a sleeping ball. "Let's be careful not to wake the other girls. Too many of us will make her nervous."

In the entryway, Mrs. Murley handed Twig her jacket and her ragged shoes. Then she opened the door and flipped on a flashlight. Still half asleep, Twig dragged her feet in the grass. Her ripped-open shoe caught on the ground and she stumbled. Mrs. Murley caught her by the hand. She didn't let it go and Twig didn't pull it away.

"I woke up, and I just had this feeling. Does that ever happen to you, Twig?"

Twig nodded, though Mrs. Murley's eyes were dancing with a joyful sort of nervousness Twig wasn't sure she'd ever felt.

"I just knew I needed to check on her, and sure enough, she was ready. Now, she might not like us watching. If she stops foaling, we'll have to give her some space. But we'll give it a try. What do you think we'll have, a colt or a filly?" Twig frowned her confusion. Mrs. Murley squeezed her hand and laughed softly. "Boy or girl?"

Twig couldn't help smiling back. "Girl," she guessed.

"Well, we'll find out soon enough."

Mrs. Murley quietly opened the door to Caper's old stall. They settled cross-legged, side by side, in the open stall door. Mystery, a curl of white in the bed of cedar shavings, lifted her head and turned her ears in their direction. But the acknowledgment lasted only long enough for Twig to see and admire the liquid determination swimming in her eyes. Then the mare turned her attention back to her task.

Mystery's nostrils flared and she twisted and thrashed and cried out, and the ponies cried back at her. Mystery stilled. Twig held her breath. The ponies quieted as though they too were holding their breath.

Mrs. Murley slipped into the stall with Mystery and whispered to the mare as she looked her over.

"What's wrong?" Twig scrambled to her feet.

"I don't know. Everything looks fine, but Mystery seems distressed."

Mystery thrashed again, less energetically, and Twig caught the darkness of fear in her eyes. She pinned her ears back and made a low sound in her throat, like a dog giving a warning growl. Mrs. Murley pulled Twig back a step.

Mystery's head drooped back down. She tucked her chin in and worry lines creased above her eyes. The still of the night, the thick of the tension, were broken by a high, thin creak.

Mrs. Murley's eyes got wide. "That was the gate."

The whites of Mystery's eyes showed, and she let out a desperate whinny, then a pleading, fear-filled scream. The ponies erupted with their own wild, nervous chorus.

"Stay here, Twig. And keep your distance, no matter what. She won't hesitate to hurt you if she thinks she's protecting her foal," she called over her shoulder as she hurried out of the stable, leaving the door open behind her in her haste.

The wind had picked up, thinning out the fog, and it blew into the stable, damp and chill.

Was she going to get Mr. Murley and his gun? What if that was the wild boy coming through the gate? What if Mr. Murley shot him? But why would he bother with the gate? He'd only opened it last time for Mystery, probably because she was too heavy with her foal to jump the fence like his stallion. What if it was someone else? Surely the wild boy wasn't alone on the island.

Twig turned her attention from the dark square of night at the end of the stable aisle to Mystery. Twig didn't move; she tried to become a part of the wall. Mystery let out a long breath, and a pair of pale forelegs emerged from her body. A head, then the foal's entire body slipped out, just like that.

Twig's hands trembled. *It* is *a miracle!* she wanted to shout to Mrs. Murley when she saw the foal raise its head. *It is!*

Mystery licked the foal clean, though it seemed to take all her energy to do so. There was a growing sort of hollow darkness in the pools of Mystery's eyes that made Twig's throat ache. But the foal turned its head toward Twig. Its mane was more a pale silver than its mother's white, and its forelock curled around a strange, white nub. Something left from the birth? A deformity? Twig leaned closer—too close for Mystery's comfort.

Mystery snorted at her, and Twig jumped back and met those quicksilver eyes, and that was when she saw it: the horn emerging from Mystery's head. It slid out slowly, bit by bit, parting her forelock. Twig's mind stumbled over the word just as her feet stumbled back another step—*unicorn*.

What other word was there for it? For a horse, white as moonlight, with mysterious pools for eyes, with the nimble cloven hooves of a deer—and now, with a lone, spiraling silvery-white horn? Could the foal's little nub be the brand-new baby beginnings of its own horn?

A quiet footfall in the silence, behind Twig. Too intentionally quiet to be one of the Murleys. Slowly, breath held, Twig turned away from Mystery and her foal.

There, with the night wind whipping his cloak out around him so that his slight frame seemed to fill the entire aisle, was the wild boy.

CHAPTER 13

THERE WAS NO MISTINESS to the wild boy. It had been mere fog, not ghostliness, in those glimpses Twig had caught before; it had belonged to the forest and to the night, not to him. The only wisping about the boy himself was his swiftness, his stealth. That was all his.

He was just a boy, not much older than Twig, but with his light brown hair and eyes that nearly matched, he looked as though he could have come right out of the earth; he was so alive and so solid, smelling of sweat and cedar and rain. How could she have ever mistaken him for a phantom?

He noticed Twig and his eyes widened in surprise, then narrowed in confusion. He hesitated a split second, like he knew he ought to run, and she realized he'd made the noise with the gate on purpose, to draw whoever was in the stable out; he hadn't counted on her being in here.

He gave Twig a fearful but determined look and brushed right past her as though he owned the place. Twig noted a bundle of sticks strapped to the boy's back, with white feathers secured to the ends. A bow slung next to them confirmed that they were arrows.

"Look what you have here, girl. A little filly." There was a slight lilting to his speech, something barely discernible and almost musical.

As he knelt next to the newborn, a leather sheath about a foot-and-a-half long stuck out from his hip. Too big to contain merely a hunting knife, it could only be a sword.

The boy spoke soothingly, but also with a clip of urgency, a quake of fear he couldn't entirely conceal. "She'll make us a fine mare, will she not, Wind Catcher?" He lay his cheek on Mystery's neck and rubbed his hand over her trembling muscles in slow, sure circles, though his eyes kept flicking to Twig and to the open stable door at the end of the aisle.

The worry lines above Mystery's eyes deepened. She whinnied, high and thin, then moaned. The ponies' voices formed a chaotic chorus of despair. The boy buried his face in the mare's mane. Twig strained to make out what he said. Something like, "He cannot give up. Not now."

"What's happening?" Twig pushed past the absolute strangeness of speaking to this boy who wasn't supposed to exist, this boy whose identity was somehow entwined with these mystery creatures who absolutely *couldn't* exist.

The boy looked up at Twig and that wildness was back in his eyes. He rose, and the wind caught his cloak again and whipped tangles of Twig's hair into her face so that she had to hold it back with both hands to see. The filly made a pitiful cry and groped at the bedding with delicate cloven hooves. Mystery's horn retracted a bit, then extended again, then retracted nearly all the way.

Mystery gave a sudden sniff-snort. She scrambled up, legs wobbling, eyes glaring at the empty aisle with desperate determination.

"No." The boy turned back to Mystery. "Don't!"

When the creature tipped her sharp horn forward and lunged out of the stall, the boy jumped back in alarm. He ran after her as she bolted out of the stable, and without thinking, Twig followed. The mare collapsed midway across the stable yard, and Twig stopped short.

"No! No!" Tears streamed down the wild boy's face. He crumpled to his knees, and his cloak spilled onto the sodden grass around him, utterly limp, no longer buoyed by the wind.

The faintest of shivers rippled over the mystery mare's body. The boy put his palm on the point of her partially extended horn and pressed it down with a shuddery sob, until it disappeared into the thick silk of her forelock.

A howl cut through the fog, and Twig ran for the stable. But the boy didn't run. He shouted a curse at the trees, said something about night, something about a dagger.

Twig stopped. She couldn't leave him out there all alone. But what could she do? She pressed herself against the outside stable wall, chest heaving. *Please, God,* she prayed. She hadn't prayed since she was six years old. No one had seemed to listen then, and probably no one was listening now, but her heart cried out anyway. *Don't let Mystery die. Don't let those things get us. Make everything right. If you're good, if you're God, make it all right.*

Tears blurred her vision, and the fog gathered thicker around the stable yard. She thought she heard hoofs galloping swiftly over the ground. She lowered her hands and blinked through the blobs of light that had formed from rubbing her eyes too hard, and tried to understand the shifting mist. Her heart skipped a beat. Some of the mist seemed to take on a horselike shape, pale and lithe and quick—just a glimpse, an impression of leaping away.

Twig searched the mist but couldn't spot Mystery or the boy. She eased back into the stable and waited by the door, wanting to shut it but afraid for the boy, that he might need to run back inside.

When the boy appeared in the stable doorway, he didn't run. He paused and grabbed a white-knuckled fistful of cloak and wiped his face, and then he looked right at Twig and came in. He was shaking violently, uncontrollably. He clutched his cloak around him, against the weather and the fear, so that Twig wanted to offer him her shell.

"You cannot tell anyone," he said hoarsely.

Twig shook her head. "I don't tell people things," she said, "just to tell people things."

He regarded her for a moment, then gave her a nod of acceptance.

"She was a unicorn," Twig whispered. "And now she's…"

She hadn't expected a reply, but the wild boy turned his

eyes on her, eyes burning with sharp, fresh grief, and he said, "Gone! She's not the only one. And if you don't take care of her"—he pointed at the filly—"it will all be for nothing."

"Me?"

"She trusted you. Her filly will too."

"But—"

He shook his head sharply. Before Twig could ask what he meant and who he was and what was going on, an eerie horse howl blew into the stable on the tail of a vicious, wet whip of wind. The boy spun on his heel and sprinted out of the stable, leaving Twig standing there in the aisle with the wakeful ponies squealing and tossing their heads on either side and the filly plaintively crying out behind her.

Twig hurried back to the stall, where the filly lay with her spindly forelegs bent up as though she had tried to use them to rise, to do something, even in her innocence and confusion. She looked at Twig with big, lonely quicksilver eyes just like Mystery's. But beside her, there was nothing but an impression in the bedding and the mess from the birth. Her mother's place was empty. Mystery was gone.

What was she going to tell Mrs. Murley about that? Mystery's little filly was still here, making it impossible for any of them to lie to themselves about Mystery's existence, to shove her into a distant corner of memory, into the cobweb of things too difficult to understand. Worse, the filly boasted her own little bit of a unicorn horn! Twig supposed it would grow as she grew, much as a deer's antlers grew as it matured. There would be no ignoring that.

Quickly, Twig crouched beside the filly. She touched her fingertip to the little horn nub. She pressed it gently, and it went down, just as Mystery's had when the wild boy had done the same. The filly laid her head in Twig's lap. Twig let her nuzzle her hand, and she rubbed her neck the way the wild boy had rubbed Mystery's, but she didn't tell her that everything was going to be all right, because there were things howling outside, and she didn't know. She just didn't know.

Mrs. Murley rushed into the stable. "I'm sorry I took so long. Casey woke up, and then Mandy and Regina. I just got them settled." She stopped short at the open stall door. "Twig? She's foaled!" Then, searching the stall and after that the stable behind her, she asked, "Where is Mystery?"

Twig licked her dry lips. She shook her head. "She's gone. I don't know. She's just—gone."

"Well, she can't have gone far, just after foaling. But why would she leave her little filly? It's just not right."

Twig burned to defend the mare. She wouldn't have left her filly if she'd had any choice. That had been clear in her final cries, her last efforts to face the threat in the woods, to protect her from it.

"Mr. Murley's outside, checking the yard. He's sure he latched that gate, but of course there's no sign of anyone—all the girls are in their beds and—I'll tell him she's missing, and then I'll be right back to have a better look at this little girl."

After Mrs. Murley ran back out, Twig got a blanket from the tack room. The filly would be cold without her mother, all alone in a great big stall. She wrapped her up, and then she settled against the inside wall of the stall and she hugged her knees to her chest and she tucked her face between her knees and she let herself cry, just for a little bit.

Twig heard Mrs. Murley coming back in, and she rubbed her face on her knees and let her hair hang in her eyes to hide their puffiness.

Mrs. Murley knelt beside the filly. "Mr. Murley's

looking for Mystery. She's got to be in the yard or the pastures somewhere. Poor little girl. I see you've got her nice and warm."

Twig didn't even try to speak around the lump in her throat. Mystery wasn't here to look after her little girl. And according to the wild boy, that meant Twig was going to have to do it. But what exactly did that mean? Feed her? Groom her? And—

Another howl rattled the night. Mrs. Murley froze for a second, then brushed it off. But Twig pushed herself up and stared into the darkness beyond the open stable doors.

She ran down the aisle and a few strides beyond, out into that darkness. She screamed, "You can't have her! You can't!" and she grabbed the stable doors and slammed them shut, first one and then the other.

She pressed against the doors, ready to put everything she had into holding them shut against whatever was out there in the deep dark of Lonehorn Island, howling and hunting the bleating little scrap of moonbeam, the silver-white filly. Her mother was more than vanished; she was gone, gone with a heavy certainty that coated Twig's heart.

But the filly was alive, a beautiful, wild, wonderful, little light. And in that moment, Twig was just as certain she'd do anything to keep it that way.

CHAPTER 14

TWIG STOOD AT THE stable door until Mrs. Murley came up behind her and pulled her shoulders to her chest and hugged her. She steered Twig back to the stall. Twig was sitting there with the filly's head in her lap when Mr. Murley came in, all wind- and sleep-rumpled.

He leaned into the stall. "So this is our new arrival. What a pretty little filly." Mrs. Murley rose, and he gave her a quick hug. "There's no sign of Mystery, and the fences are all undamaged."

"It's dark. I'm sure we'll find her in the morning."

Twig spoke up. She nodded at the filly. "I think she's hungry."

"I'm sure she is," Mr. Murley said. "Hungry and confused."

Mrs. Murley pulled her collar up and put her hands in her pockets. "I'll be right back."

She returned a few minutes later with a bowl of milk and a rag. "Hold her head in your lap, Twig, and we'll see if we can get her to eat. Come on, wild one. I know it's not what you want, but it's all we've got."

Twig dipped the rag in the milk herself and offered it to the filly.

"What should we call our little wild one?"

"Wild one," Twig repeated absently, thinking more of the boy now than the filly. Who had he run to? Who would he tell about what had happened to Mystery? Twig realized she was no longer wondering who else was out there for her own curiosity, even for her own safety—she was wondering for the boy. The boy whose fear and grief had been every bit as real as his body once he came out of the shadows and stood in the faint glow of the dimmed stable lights.

"Yes," Mrs. Murley said, "Wild One. Let's call her Wild One."

But Twig's heart said, *No, she's a silver-white sliver of light in the darkest night.* "She should have *Light* in her name."

Mrs. Murley smiled. "Wild Light, then. What a beautiful name for our little filly."

"I'll have to go to the vet in the morning to get some supplies so we can feed her," Mr. Murley said.

Twig stopped, letting the rag drip down the front of her jacket. The filly nuzzled the stream of milk. "You can't let the vet see her."

Mr. Murley ran a finger over one of Wild Light's little cloven hooves. "No, I suppose we can't. Twig…"

He didn't say anything more, but his eyes said, *There's more, isn't there? More that you know.*

•••

Twig heard Mrs. Murley whispering to Casey to let her sleep. The memory of what had happened before Mrs. Murley ushered her to bed in the still-dark hours of the morning, assuring her that Mr. Murley would watch Wild Light, filtered through Twig's fatigue. She threw the covers off and shrugged away Mrs. Murley's protests. Twig slipped into her old shoes rather than taking the time to fumble with her boots, and followed the girls to the stable for early morning chores.

The girls were all murmuring about the filly and about

Mystery's disappearance. Twig was quiet as she followed Casey's directions and fed Rain Cloud. She peeked at Wild Light real quick, but there were too many people poking around her and Mr. Murley, asking too many questions.

With the ponies fed, Mr. Murley shooed the girls out of the stable. Twig was the last one out, and she lingered on the path, gazing at the woods. How safe was the little filly, even in the daylight?

At the edge of the pasture beyond the stable yard, movement flickered in the trees—movement that seemed to want her attention just as much as it wanted to be hidden. Movement that now made her want to stay, just as much as yesterday it had made her want to run. The wild boy.

"Come on, Twig," Taylor called as Twig drifted closer to the pasture.

Twig shoved her hands in her pockets and tipped her head to the morning sky, trying to give the impression that she was just enjoying having a look at the day wakening over the island.

"It's breakfast," Casey added with a frown.

"Just a minute."

Taylor sighed and took Casey's hand and tugged her

toward the house. When they were far enough away, Twig ran for the pasture gate, and darted across the wet grass and behind one of the pony shelters. She stepped up to the fence line and stood still and waited. The boy's face emerged.

"The filly," he whispered. His eyes, reddened and shadowed, were full of questions and fear.

"She's okay." Twig twisted her toe in the damp earth. "She's beautiful."

The boy smiled a small, sad, longing smile.

Twig looked down uncomfortably, and that was when she saw his hands. "What happened to you?"

He held out his muddied, bloodied hands, as if noticing them for the first time. His face got hard, then crumpled. He crossed his arms, stuffing his dirty, trembling hands under his cloak.

"They're after you, aren't they?" She nodded toward the woods behind him.

Twig took his silence for a yes. She wanted to grab his cloak and take him into the house and feed him hot chocolate and pancakes with apple cider syrup.

"I thought you were with them at first," she said.

"Not now. But…it's complicated."

"You can tell me. Maybe I can help." What had possessed her to say that? What could *she* do?

He shook his head, so she shifted back to something more pleasant. "We named the filly Wild Light."

"A good name for such a wonder."

"A wonder?" Twig recalled something she'd read, a line about great signs and wonders. "You mean like a miracle?"

"Is that what you call it here?"

Twig shook her head. "I'd call a unicorn magic, here or anywhere else."

The boy raised his eyebrows. He folded his arms again. "There's not a bit magic about unicorns."

"What about their horns?"

"That's just how they're made."

Twig raised her eyebrows right back. He didn't think horns that appeared and disappeared were magic? She shouldn't be surprised. This strange boy might have grown up on the island, learning nothing more than what the woods had to teach him.

"*Miracle*," he whispered. "I like that word." He was looking at his hands again. "My father's gone too. I was digging. The ground was so hard…"

He pulled his cloak tighter around him and shrank back into the brush.

"Your father?" Had he been here with the boy, on the island? And now that he was gone, was the boy all alone?

"Twig?" It was Janessa's voice, calling from the stable yard.

The Murleys had probably sent Janessa after her. She should go. But seeing the boy melting back into the shadows alone—

She clambered over the fence.

He stopped, startled, then turned his back on her. Twig wanted to hide in her shell, until he looked over his shoulder and said, "Are you not coming?"

CHAPTER 15

TWIG SLIPPED AFTER THE boy. She hadn't meant to go anywhere, not really; she'd just wanted to—well, she wasn't entirely sure what she'd intended to do when she jumped over that fence. Make sure he was okay, somehow. She should go back. But before Twig could figure out a way to make her excuses, they came to a hollow under the trees.

In that hollow was a little shelter built of evergreen branches propped against a tree—and next to it, the wild boy's stallion. His ears pricked up at Twig, his nose out, nostrils slightly flared, neck arched—the body language that Mrs. Murley had told Twig meant a pony or a horse was curious and eager to meet a new creature.

"This is Indigo Independence. He's—he was Wind Catcher's mate."

His coat was the palest of gray, his mane and tail a shade darker. Slowly, Twig extended a hand toward him. He gave her a sniff, then stepped back, his curiosity satisfied. She was merely a harmless, scrawny girl, his eyes seemed to say. He kept an ear tuned to her, but he turned his attention to the boy, giving him a nudge of reserved affection. The stallion carried himself with an intelligence, a knowing sort of pride—the pride of one whose prowess had been tested.

This was little Wild Light's father. Would she grow up to be like him?

"I call him Indy," the boy said.

At first Twig thought he was just stroking the horse's forelock, but then the boy said, "Let's show her your horn, shall we?"

It rose under his palm, slowly spiraling, rougher, stronger, longer than Wind Catcher's. A fine, deep blue stripe followed the spiral.

"Unicorns aren't as big as most horses, but they are more agile, more swift, and they have these." He nodded at the horn. "They aren't just for show."

"The noises in the woods…?"

"Unicorns. There aren't many; they don't produce many young, but when they do, they grow quickly, and if nothing happens to them, they live long." He gave Twig a piercing look. "You must make sure his filly is used to human contact. Unicorns are naturally wild—wilder than horses. We cannot afford for her to grow up wild."

What? Who exactly did this boy think he was? Who did he think *she* was? "But I—I might not be here long. The Murleys aren't my parents."

"You're not a Murley?"

"No."

The boy frowned. "You're just visiting?"

"Well...not exactly. They're my guardians, for now."

The boy lifted his chin as though he'd already won the argument. "One year—less, I think—and she'll be ready to ride. She'll be nearly grown, not like a horse."

"I don't know anything about horses anyway. I don't—"

"Never mind, then," he snapped. He took a clump of Indy's mane in his hand and leaped effortlessly onto his back.

He couldn't go, not yet. Not like that. "What's your name?" Twig said in a rush.

"Ben."

"Ben what?"

"Just Ben."

"Oh." Twig didn't know what she'd expected, but certainly something less normal than *Ben*. "Everybody calls me Twig."

He scowled and looked as though he were trying to decide whether it was worth his while to care what her name was.

"I'll be here for a year," Twig said, trying not to think of Daddy. "At least. We're throwaway girls, all of us. The Murleys have us because nobody else who can take care of us wants us right now. I'll be here. I guess I can help."

He peered down at her from under shaggy bangs. He dismounted, walked over to her, and folded his arms. Awkwardly, Twig folded hers too.

"They killed my father," he said, barely above a whisper. "My father," he said louder, deeper, "who devoted his life to protecting them from each other, from people who would use them and destroy them. He taught me to do the same. He was Wind Catcher's rider. He tamed her, and when she chose Indigo Independence for her mate, I tamed him too, even though he was the fiercest, the wildest yearling my father ever saw."

His voice lifted with admiration for a father who was now gone. "We guarded the island from intruders and kept its secret, just as the herders have always done. But they never had Dagger to deal with."

"Dagger?" Twig scrunched deeper into her shell at the way Ben said that name.

"Midnight Dagger. When he was born, my father named him Midnight Dream. Indy's horn has a twist of blue." Ben traced his finger along that fine stripe in the grooves of the spiral. "But Midnight Dream's entire horn is a deep midnight blue. When he turned to killing, Midnight Dream became Midnight Dagger."

"Killing?"

Ben nodded. "Dagger is the leader of Lonehorn Island's herd. They follow him because he's strong in body, strong in spirit. But that spirit took a dark turn, and the others still followed his lead. When the Murleys came, and then all you girls, things got even more complicated."

"They want to be left alone."

"Unicorns are very territorial. They'll kill another herd,

down to the last foal, over territory. Herders keep the peace between them. Lonehorn Island's herd has always known and accepted herders with their tame unicorns. They've never seen us as a threat. But Dagger started…"

"Tell me. Please."

"They're omnivorous. They can eat plants or meat. But the more flesh in their diet, the more they crave it. Too much of it and sometimes they become aggressive, not just fighting to protect their territory and their young, but becoming predators, active at night instead of during the day. In rare cases, they begin killing just to kill."

Twig stared wide-eyed at Indy's horn, imagining what a predator could do with such a weapon.

"We feared for the ponies on the ranch and for what would happen to any of you if you tried to defend them from an attack. We set up camp just outside the ranch. When we drove Dagger back, shooting one of his herd and wounding him, he turned against us. Once he'd healed, he came after us."

Ben blinked hard. Indy nuzzled him, and he buried his face in his mane.

"Who else is here?" Twig whispered. "With you, I mean."

Ben raised his head. "Just Indy now. The others all follow Dagger."

"I mean *people*."

"Oh. I lived…somewhere else. With my father. We spent a lot of time here, but we had to go home to…take care of some things. When we came back to the island, things were bad. Dagger and some of the others had gotten so bold, so vicious, they jumped the fence and attacked a horse in the pasture."

Caper! "Casey—one of the other girls—she says they ate him."

Ben didn't deny it. "Dagger came after Wind Catcher, and Indy fought him, but I wouldn't let Indy finish him off. I couldn't stop thinking about the one I'd shot and killed the last time. I took an oath to protect unicorns." He shook his head and his eyes filled with tears of regret. "My father was riding Wind Catcher, and he was injured in the fight. I had to get him out of there. That was all I could think of. But he died anyway, and now Dagger's still out there. When he's strong enough, he'll be back."

"All that happened because of us, because the Murleys brought us girls here."

"It's not your fault. Dagger is the reason my father's gone, and Wind Catcher too…"

Indy rubbed up against Ben, and Ben whispered back affectionately.

"It's nothing like the fairy tales, is it? They say only a maiden can tame the unicorn."

"It isn't true. I looked Indy in the eye. I touched his horn. I dared to say his name and to teach him to answer to it." He paused, blinking hard. It was a while before he met her eyes again. When he did, the faraway look was gone.

"They said Mr. Murley built a higher fence after what happened to Caper. But you jumped it with Indy, didn't you?"

"Indy's a spectacular jumper. He's a natural, but I've also trained him to jump higher and farther. The others cannot jump it. But if they're determined enough, they'll find a way to get what they want."

Twig cringed.

"Twig!"

Twig jumped and Ben stiffened. The shout was closer this time, and it was Mr. Murley, not just one of the girls.

"Go," said Ben gruffly. "Someone wants you."

Twig ran back. Mr. Murley stood at the fence. When he saw her, a smile replaced his look of concern.

"Let's go, Twig, before they eat all the waffles."

Waffles! She clambered over the fence, feeling a strange ache inside.

"Twig," Mr. Murley said as they walked side by side, "you need to stay inside the fence. It's not safe to go into the woods alone."

Ben was in the woods alone—with his bow and his sword and Indy, yes, but still alone. Standing between them and a herd of wild unicorns that would soon be on the hunt again.

CHAPTER 16

AFTER BREAKFAST AND CHORES, Twig tiptoed to Wild Light's stall. Mr. Murley was in there, his lap covered in spilled milk, trying to feed her.

"Hi there, Twig." He grinned and started to rise, but Wild Light wobbled up too, bumping him back onto his bottom in her newborn clumsiness.

Twig laughed softly as Wild Light tried to suckle Mr. Murley's milk-soaked shirttail.

"Can I try?"

"Sure. Maybe she'll find you less distracting, since you're not covered in her lunch."

"Yet," Twig said. Then she blushed, feeling dumb. What was she doing laughing, joking?

Mr. Murley smiled and handed her the rag. "See what you can get down her. I've got to get into town and buy some supplies to feed her properly."

Mr. Murley left Twig alone with Wild Light. The filly steadied herself, then hopped straight up in the air, all four hooves off the ground, right in front of Twig. Twig yelped in surprise. Wild Light had only jumped a few inches, but it was such a funny, rabbitlike bounce.

She nuzzled expectantly at Twig.

"Calm down, now. I know you're hungry, but you're going to have to be still if you want anything to eat."

Twig pushed gently on Wild Light's rump, and the filly folded her legs under her. Soon, Wild Light was half in Twig's lap, the bowl of milk was spilled, and she was sucking milk drips from Twig's hair.

Casey peeked around the stall door. "Wow. She's a messy eater. I'm supposed to tell you it's time to learn how to halter Rain Cloud."

Twig rose, gently nudging Wild Light off. When Twig turned her back on the filly, she cried pitifully.

"She doesn't want you to leave, does she?"

Twig didn't want to leave Wild Light either. It didn't seem right for such a new baby to be all alone.

"I know," Casey said. "We'll halter them both!"

"I don't know…" What if the wild unicorns were just

waiting for her to come outside? But Ben *had* said she needed to be tamed.

In a moment, Casey had Rain Cloud by the halter and Twig had the prancing little Wild Light in the aisle. Casey led Rain Cloud to Wild Light and the pony and the unicorn stood nose to nose. Before Twig could stop her, Wild Light danced playfully around Rain Cloud. She jumped, her leap verging on a rear, right in the pony's face.

Twig heard a gasp of alarm. Mrs. Murley had entered the stable, and her eyes were big and round. But Rain Cloud just gave the filly one of his indignant snorts, then a glare of warning. Wild Light retreated a step and gave an *I'm sorry—I got too excited* whinny.

Mrs. Murley took hold of Rain Cloud and led him away from Wild Light. "Girls," she said sternly, "that filly is too young for a halter."

"I'm sorry," Casey said. "I should've asked, huh?"

"I know it's exciting having a newborn filly, but we have to be careful to keep her safe. And introducing a new animal to a pony is a big deal. It can be dangerous."

"We didn't want to leave Wild Light alone," Twig said.

"I know. And she might cry when you go, but she really

needs to get some rest. Let's put her back, and when Mr. Murley comes home with a bottle and some formula for her, you can help feed her again. It's time for you girls to groom your ponies now."

•••

Twig stood in the pasture, watching Rain Cloud and the other ponies. Taylor's pony, a golden-colored mare named Chatterbox, trotted up to greet Rain Cloud. Rain Cloud's ears pricked toward Chatterbox, and he nickered softly at her. He looked peaceful enough when he was with his friends, away from Twig.

"How's the filly?" Regina said, trying to sound nonchalant.

"Lonely."

"I wonder what happened to her mom." Regina was quiet for a second. Then, "My mom's in jail," she said.

Regina was waiting for her to say something, maybe to ask, *For what?* Maybe to say, *Mine too*. But Twig didn't feel like saying anything. She didn't know if her mom even knew where she was. Twig had sent her a letter just before what happened to Emily. Would she write back? If she did, would Keely answer it for her? Would she tell her what she'd done with Twig?

Maybe, in jail, Mom would be clean enough to care. Maybe. Mom hadn't put up much of a fuss when the police came. After they took her away, the police had found Daddy, and Daddy had wanted Twig. He'd been looking for her. He'd hugged her and called her *Twig*, in that way that made her love being Twig. But Daddy had come with Keely.

Mrs. Murley approached the girls. "Let's go get Rain Cloud's tack ready, Twig," she said, "and then I'll show you how we catch him and get him saddled up."

Mrs. Murley laid some sort of padding and a saddle in Twig's arms. It was much heavier than Twig expected, and her skinny, worn-to-wobbling arms nearly dropped it.

Mrs. Murley pretended not to notice as she draped an incomprehensible tangle of leather straps over her own arm. "I've been riding Rain Cloud. He'll be glad to have a break from such a heavy burden."

Twig would be glad to have a break from heavy loads herself, but not if it meant riding Rain Cloud, who'd probably spent the last hour in the pasture plotting and laughing his snorty pony laugh with his friends about how he was going to send the new girl flying. Twig considered tossing her armload up in the air and making a run for it. Maybe there was some more poo for her to scoop up, another wheelbarrow to dump.

Twig nodded every now and then as Mrs. Murley demonstrated how to saddle Rain Cloud. She followed dutifully as she led the pony out to the stable yard.

And then Mrs. Murley said, "Now just put your toe in the stirrup and hold on there."

Twig considered refusing. Didn't ponies bite? How far back could Rain Cloud's mouth reach? Regina was smirking at her. But Rain Cloud seemed tame enough, and she didn't want to look like a total wuss. Twig grabbed the pommel and put her slippery-soled, pointy toe in the stirrup and hauled herself up. She peeked at the ground. Not too far. Thank God Keely had gotten her into a pony ranch and not that horse ranch in Texas that Twig had seen when she pulled up Keely's Internet search history.

With Rain Cloud's lead in hand, Mrs. Murley said something to the pony and started to walk them slowly around the yard. Rain Cloud trotted forward. Twig squeezed her thighs and tried not to flinch. Falling wouldn't be so bad, as long as she didn't get trampled. Mrs. Murley was saying something about the reins, but Twig was busy planning how she'd ninja roll to safety if it came to that.

"Twig, honey, just relax your legs and hold the reins nice and gentle. When you squeeze, he thinks you want him to go faster."

Twig stopped squeezing. The last thing she wanted was for Rain Cloud to go faster.

CHAPTER 17

"ARE YOU READY, TWIG?" Mr. Murley said.

Twig took a deep breath. She wasn't, not really, but Wild Light needed her. At first, Mr. Murley had taken care of Wild Light, but he'd let Twig bottle-feed her, and though she'd figured Mr. Murley would want the filly for himself since Caper was gone, he'd stepped aside, quietly and gradually letting Twig take on the responsibility for Wild Light.

Twig had worried that Wild Light's horn would pop up like Pinocchio's nose and give her away, but there had been no sign of it since the day she was born. What if she wasn't caring for her right and it wasn't growing at all? What would she tell Ben when he came back for her—if he came back for her? There hadn't been a glimpse of him since the day after Wild Light was born, since he'd introduced her to Indy.

The filly was just two weeks old, but she was already bouncing off her stall walls—sometimes literally. She could spring up in the air nearly to the height of Twig's shoulders without a running start. Today, they were going to turn her out for the first time, and that meant introducing her to the ponies. Twig willed her hand not to tremble as she held Wild Light's halter. What if they didn't like her? She was so different.

Mr. Murley said, "Remember, girls, we have to watch very closely. Wild Light doesn't know how to behave in a herd, and she doesn't have a mare to protect her. I think she's sure enough on her feet to get out of the way if there's trouble, but...if she does something one of the others doesn't want to tolerate, she could get hurt."

"I'll keep hold of Sparkler," Mandy offered. "She *is* the alpha mare. She's not gonna like this."

Janessa rolled her eyes at Mandy, but followed her out to the pasture to wait with the ponies for Wild Light's entrance.

Wild Light skipped along the aisle toward the sunlight and open air, eager and carefree. Though Twig had her by the halter, it was clear she wasn't in the lead.

"Celeste!"

Twig turned at Regina's cry. Celeste was charging right at Wild Light—until Rain Cloud intercepted her. Celeste hesitated as Rain Cloud blocked her path, but the determination to run Wild Light off was still in her eyes. And then Sparkler intervened. All it took was a look from the alpha mare, and Celeste retreated.

"No, Celeste!" Regina took hold of her pony. "That's not nice!"

"Don't be too hard on her," Mr. Murley said. "She's at the low end of the pecking order. She wants to show Wild Light her dominance, so she won't be at the bottom anymore."

Regina's forehead creased with a compassion Twig had never seen in her before, and she whispered reassurances to her pony.

With an impish whinny, Wild Light hopped and grabbed Gadget's tail, giving it a little yank-nip. Gadget whinnied his outrage and kicked at Wild Light, but the filly sprang back just in time, and Rain Cloud stepped forward once again to defend her.

Janessa calmed her pony while Mr. Murley took Rain Cloud by the halter, and Twig fumbled in a vain attempt to get hold of Wild Light again.

Wild Light scampered behind Rain Cloud, then peeked around him and gave Gadget what could only be a look of defiance. *Ha! I can do whatever I want!*

But Rain Cloud gave the filly an admonishing nip, and Wild Light bent her head down apologetically. Relieved to have her still for a moment, Twig grasped Wild Light's halter. Mr. Murley had her take the filly into the next paddock, where she could taunt the ponies through the fence instead.

Twig leaned on the ponies' side of the fence, watching the little bolt of white test her legs. Rain Cloud nuzzled up to Twig, and she scratched his head. "You're a good boy," she whispered. "I'm proud of you."

Mr. Murley came and stood next to Twig. "Well, it's going to take a while, but I think she'll find her place all right."

Twig caught a hint of uncertainty in Mr. Murley's tone. He was watching Wild Light hop. Watching the way she held her head high. Her strange gait, so unlike a horse—like a creature meant for something other than a pasture, something wilder. She might find a way to get along while she was small. But she was growing and maturing so fast. And Twig had a feeling no alpha pony would be able to keep a grown Wild Light in line. No fence would keep her in.

May

CHAPTER 18

TWIG PAUSED TO STRAIGHTEN Rain Cloud's name-plate. She'd painted his name in pale blue, cursive letters. She glanced at Wild Light's stall. It still said "Caper." Wild Light stuck her head over the stall door and watched Twig pour the feed into Rain Cloud's bin, as she'd done every morning for nearly two months. Rain Cloud dug into his breakfast with his usual noisy appreciation.

"Twig!" Janessa came jogging in. "Mrs. M needs you right away!"

"Okay. Be right back, Rainy-boy. Hang on, Wild Light."

Wild Light whickered her protest, but Rain Cloud just rotated an ear toward her. The rest of him stayed focused on breakfast. He was a good pony. Now that Twig knew a thing or two about ponies, she realized just how easy he was.

Twig jogged toward the front door. Mrs. Murley was standing on the porch, waving her in. It was Saturday morning, and she supposed Mrs. Murley wanted her help with breakfast. She'd gotten pretty good with the apple cider syrup.

Mrs. Murley called to her again. "Hurry, Twig!"

Twig hurried, imagining lumpy syrup or some other breakfast emergency. But Mrs. Murley steered her toward the office instead. Twig held back, confused. The girls weren't allowed in there, not without special permission.

"Go on, Twig, there's someone here who wants to talk to you."

"Here?"

"There." Mrs. Murley pointed to the laptop, sitting open on her desk.

Twig's heart stopped, then started again double time. A blurry image moved on the screen. A face. Daddy. Twig sank into the chair in front of the screen.

"Twig," Daddy said, "how are you doing, baby?"

Oh, Daddy, you're so far away. That was all Twig could think, but she couldn't say it, or she'd cry. And she couldn't cry or she'd never stop. She bolted up, sending the office chair rolling into the wall, and she ducked under Mrs. Murley's arm and ran for her bedroom.

A minute later Mrs. Murley came in and shut the door softly behind her. "Twig?"

Twig's head was buried in her pillow, but she felt Mrs. Murley sink onto the bed beside her.

"Oh, Twig." She brushed her hair with her hand. "I'm sorry. He just messaged me. I knew I should've talked to you first, but he insisted. He was afraid you'd say no again if I asked. You haven't spoken to him in months, Twig... I'm sorry."

Twig turned her face slightly to the side and peeked at Mrs. Murley through her tangles. She'd pulled her neat ponytail out at the same time she'd thrown herself onto the bed. How could she explain why she couldn't talk to him now? Now that he knew she'd turned bad like Mom. Now that he'd let Keely send her away.

"Maybe sometime," Mrs. Murley said tentatively, "you could tell me about your dad. He misses you. You could write him a letter instead."

Twig shoved her face back into the pillow. He didn't miss *this* Twig. He missed the little girl she used to be.

"Or just draw a picture?"

Twig lifted her head. Daddy had loved her drawings when she was small, when things were different. But she was too old for crayons and drippy paintings now.

"Those sketches you did for our botany study were beautiful, Twig. I'll bet your dad would love to see something like that."

"I wouldn't have to say anything?"

"Not a word." Mrs. Murley smiled. "A picture is worth a thousand, and all that."

CHAPTER 19

RAIN CLOUD LET OUT an impatient breath, making Twig's hair tickle the back of her neck.

"Be good. I'm almost done." Twig patted him absently, then went back to darkening the shadows beneath the wild violets she was sketching at the edge of the meadow.

Maybe she'd send this one to Daddy too. Yesterday she'd gotten a letter from him, telling her he'd gotten her drawings, all of plants growing on the island. She'd felt like the old Twig he'd loved.

But was that who she was anymore? One day he'd come back and he'd realize she was still the snapped-in-half Twig. The Twig that had seen and done too many bad things. Then what?

"Aaah!" a shriek from the edge of the woods interrupted the quiet footsteps and laughter of the girls in the meadow, the nickers and tail swishes of their ponies. "Look!" Taylor said.

Twig dropped her sketchbook and plunged through the ferns with Mrs. Murley and the other girls.

"Ew!" Janessa scrunched her eyes shut.

Mandy reached for Casey's hand. Regina looked pale.

At their feet were the remains of a raccoon. But that wasn't all. Around it, the brush had been trampled. Leaves were marked with blood.

"What do you think did it?" Taylor asked Mrs. Murley.

"Maybe we have a mountain lion here on the island," Mrs. Murley said.

Stomach churning, Twig bent down and examined the ground. It wasn't marred by paw prints; it was gouged with the distinctive pattern of hooves—cloven hooves. Taylor knelt next to her.

"A deer?" She looked questioningly at Twig.

Twig shrugged, but her heart was pounding. She took a big step back. "Come on. Let's get out of here."

"Yeah," Regina said. "This is gross."

Twig ran for the open sky and the tall meadow grass.

She stuffed her sketchbook in her backpack and mounted Rain Cloud.

Maybe when they got back, she'd try to slip away to Ben's hollow and look for him again. She'd only checked for him there once and found the hollow empty. Then she'd worried that she would be followed there and he'd be discovered.

The hungry howls had died down after the night Wild Light was born, but they'd come back a few nights ago. Distant, but for how long? Now she knew that Dagger wasn't gone. But was Ben? Sometimes she thought about riding Rain Cloud off the trails and looking for Ben. Rain Cloud minded Twig now, and Twig rode well enough too. But Rain Cloud wouldn't veer off the path into the woods. None of the ponies would, not for Twig or for anyone else.

Sometimes, when she was standing at the stove stirring the syrup and watching Mrs. Murley drop pancake batter onto the electric skillet, she wanted to tell her about Ben. She imagined Mrs. Murley's concern, her sending Mr. Murley after Ben, then Mr. Murley bringing him inside, where it was warm. But something told her Ben would not be found. And he wouldn't come if he were. For so long,

Twig hadn't wanted to tell people things. Now she had people she wanted to tell, and too many things she had to keep secret instead—the truth about what had happened to her stepsister, Emily. The unicorns. Ben.

June

Chapter 20

TWIG LEANED AGAINST THE corner of Wild Light's stall, balancing her sketchbook against her chest. "Stay right there, girl. That's good."

Wild Light was grown enough that Twig had to lift her chin up a little to look into her eyes. She was strong and sleek and beautiful, and still pure white, except for her pale silver-gray mane and tail.

Twig had learned that when it came to drawing, white was more than just white. Slowly, gradually, she shaded the shadows that defined Wild Light's shape. Twig took her gum eraser from the pocket of her shell and rubbed at a highlight that had gotten smudged, to make it whiter again. She blew off the eraser bits, stuck the ebony pencil in her mouth, and used her fingertips to blend the soft, dark graphite and smooth the edge between shadow and highlight.

Wild Light's ears perked up, and she nickered—her nicker that meant, *Hello. Hello, friend.* Twig heard the stable door shut. She frowned. She'd been concentrating so hard on her drawing, she'd missed the sound of it opening. Who would be out here this late? Mr. and Mrs. Murley knew she was in the stable sketching. Maybe it was later than she thought and they'd sent one of the girls to get her. She lowered her pencil and peered over the stall wall.

Ben's light brown eyes stared back at her. She dropped her pencil in the wood shavings.

"Hi," she managed to say.

"Hello." He pushed the hood of his cloak back. His hair was longer now, though the ends of the waves looked like someone had sawed at them with a knife. "I come in here at night sometimes, to see her. When no one else is here."

"Me too."

He gestured at the stall door with his head. "Can I come in?"

"Oh." Twig tucked her sketchbook under her arm and reached for the latch, but he opened it himself first.

Wild Light went right to him and nuzzled his head.

Ben laughed softly and rubbed her neck. "Wild Light," Ben whispered in her ear. "This Twig girl wasn't born a herder, but she'll make you a good enough rider just the same, I think."

Herder? Rider? Twig wanted to ask Ben what he meant; she wanted to ask him so many things. But his attention was focused on Wild Light. He whispered to her and listened to her soft, breathy answers, and Twig knew better, after these months at Island Ranch, than to interrupt that sort of conversation.

When he and Wild Light were done talking, Ben plucked the pencil out of the bedding and handed it to Twig. "Can I see?" He gestured at the sketchbook.

Twig shrugged. Before, she would've refused. Now that she was used to the girls peeking over her shoulder all the time, she felt only the slightest knot in her stomach as she folded the sketchbook cover back and held it out to Ben.

He studied the drawing and one corner of his mouth turned up. She'd drawn Wild Light leaping, dancelike. She'd been sketching her at play in the pasture most of the day, and now she'd come in here with her for a closer look, to fill in the details on her final drawing—the drawing she was going to send to Daddy. It was something more than flowers and leaves this time. Something new.

"It's amazing," Ben said, "but something's missing."

Oh. "What?"

Ben passed the sketchbook back to her. He reached his hands up to Wild Light's head, worked his fingers through the silky mass of her forelock, and rubbed them in a circular motion.

A white tip poked through the forelock. Slowly, it lengthened, turning as it did so, like a twist of rope unwinding. It was pure white.

"Her horn! I kept expecting it to pop out like magic, but it never did."

Ben smiled a crooked, impish little smile, looking, just for an instant, like a very different boy. "I told you, it's not magic. It's retractable. See how her head curves up a little higher than your ponies'? There's an extra space there. The horn is hollow. Most of it slides within itself, and it pulls back into that space—the cornal cavity."

Twig's mouth dropped open. *Cornal cavity?*

"Don't worry," Ben assured her. "I can coax it back down."

"I did that," Twig recalled in a whisper. "After her mother died. I saw you do it with Mys—with Wind Catcher."

He nodded. "They only extend their horns when they're around other unicorns, but they'll let a rider draw it out or ease it in if he asks right."

"Why'd she let me?"

"She trusted you," Ben said, as though that were obvious.

Twig felt a brief flicker of pride but quickly checked it. Wild Light had been so new to the world then, so alone and afraid, she probably would have trusted anyone.

Twig put her hand on the side of the horn; she was afraid that if she touched the end of it, she might accidentally push it, and it would go down again. She traced the slight ribbing that spiraled around it with her finger. It was so smooth, almost sharp. Ben let her admire it in peace.

After a minute, she stood back and opened her sketchbook to a fresh page and she sketched just the horn. It wasn't so bad, drawing with Ben there. He was quiet, and he looked at Wild Light, not at her.

"I'll add it to the drawing of Wild Light tomorrow," she said. "I'll show you—if I see you again."

"You'll see me. Soon."

Then he took her hand and placed it on the tip of the horn. "Go on. Just a little push."

That was all it took, just a gentle, steady pressure, until the horn disappeared into Wild Light's forelock, and she was something unnameable again.

"I'd better go," Ben said. "Indy gets impatient."

"He probably worries about you," Twig said, then blushed and ducked her head quickly, afraid she'd revealed her own concern.

"Of course he does," Ben said matter-of-factly. "There's enough to worry about. For anybody," he added.

Twig looked back up, but this time Ben was avoiding her eyes. "I have to go too," she said. "To go in."

"I'll see you." Ben pulled his cloak around him and swept out of the stable into the night, alone. At least he had Indy. That was something. Much more than she'd realized it could be before she'd gotten to know Wild Light.

As Twig headed back to the house, she considered adding the horn to the drawing in her room tonight. Casey wouldn't complain if she turned on her flashlight. Once the drawing was done, she'd be able to see Wild Light as she was meant to be, whenever she wanted.

No, the Murleys were waiting to look at it, and all the girls wanted to see it. If they saw that picture of Wild Light with her horn, would they think Twig just had an imagination, or would that be just what it took for them to understand what Wild Light really was? She couldn't risk that.

She could draw Wild Light with her horn, but she'd have to wait until after she showed them the drawing without it. Then she'd have Mrs. Murley make some copies of the drawing with the printer, and she'd use one of them, along with her sketches of the horn, to draw a new, complete picture of Wild Light with her horn.

CHAPTER 21

TWIG KNELT ON THE cool, wet sand beside the other girls. They were writing their names in the sand with their fingers. She traced the outline of a unicorn instead. Even in the mid-June sun, the sand was cold and it hurt when it ground too far under her nails, so Twig headed for the tree line to find a stick.

Mr. and Mrs. Murley knelt on a blanket on the dry sand farther up the beach, packing what was left of the picnic. With their schoolwork done for the year, they'd all decided to take a hike after their morning chores, rather than riding.

They'd climbed up to Bald Peak, the highest point on the island. The steep hill was capped with smooth rock, free of trees, offering a stunning view of the shoreline and of Cedar Harbor beyond. Twig had turned to head back down the slope and taken in the view of the island itself. A mass of fog covered the interior of the island. On the sunniest of days, in the deep of the woods, Lonehorn Island was still Lonehorn Island.

Twig bent to pick up a stick but quickly stood when she glimpsed movement in the woods. The movement stopped, and Twig wondered if it was only wishful thinking. Then she saw it again—a hand raised, partly obscured by the brush. It had to be Ben. Twig dropped the stick.

"I'm going to go over there and read, okay?" she called to the Murleys, loud enough that Ben could hear. She pointed to an outcrop of rock about a hundred yards away.

"Sure, Twig," Mr. Murley said. "Just don't go so far you can't hear us, okay?"

"Okay."

Twig ran across the sand, barefoot, and scrambled up the rough rock, then slowed down to step carefully around the slippery black areas, where sea urchins and barnacles waited for the tide to come in. She slid down the other side of the rock and into the sand.

Ben was right there, waiting. He stepped back

awkwardly. It was strange to see him out in the open, in the sunshine. He seemed different than he had in the stable.

"Hi," Twig made herself say.

"Hi. I heard you say you were coming over here to read. Is that what you keep in there? Books?"

Twig never showed anyone what was in her backpack. Most of the girls had never asked. The others only asked once. But Ben's eyes were red, like he'd been crying.

She took off her backpack, stepped into a niche in the rock, and sat down on the sand. "No one can see us here. We'll hear them coming first."

He sat beside her, and she took out the only book in her backpack, a little Bible Mr. Murley had given her, and laid it on the sand.

He nodded at it. "I had a lot of my own books, back home."

It was difficult to imagine Ben having a home other than the island, to imagine Ben sitting indoors, reading a book. She opened the backpack and took out a carefully folded piece of paper. She'd made just one copy of this drawing; she'd had to sneak into the Murleys' office to do it.

"It's for you."

"Thanks."

Ben unfolded the paper and held it up in the sunlight. Wild Light danced across the page. Twig had shaded the sky around her, so she could show the light glinting off the point of her horn. Sometimes she imagined it was sunlight, sometimes moonlight.

"Wow," Ben said.

"I wish I could see her, just like that. Leaping in the pasture, but with her horn."

"Me too. And I wish my father could see her."

Ben let his hair fall over his face. He folded the picture back up and set it aside.

"Want to see a picture of my dad?" Twig regretted the words as soon as they left her mouth. His dad was dead; why would he want to see hers?

But Ben said, "Sure."

Twig took the portrait of Daddy in his dress uniform from her backpack and handed it to Ben. Then she took out a bright orange fishing lure and a picture of her and Mom all dressed up. Daddy wasn't in that picture because he'd taken it. His princesses, he'd called them. And she'd really felt like one that day.

She told Ben about the first fish she'd caught with

Daddy. She told him about the fancy dinner he'd treated them to for her fifth birthday, right after Daddy took that picture. Ben leaned in intently as she spoke, and then he leaned back against the rocks in a satisfied way when she was finished.

"Those are great stories, Twig."

She nodded. He believed them. He believed them because they were true. It was so hard for them to feel true to her anymore. He handed back the pictures and the fishing lure, and her eyes wandered to the leather pack at his hip. She'd never noticed it before. His cloak had always covered it.

He saw her looking and said, "I don't have any stories in there. Just lunch." He picked up the Bible. "I miss stories."

"You can have it. You must get…bored." *Lonely,* she'd almost said, but she didn't want to embarrass him. "Besides, you like miracles, and that's what it's about—miracles."

Ben slipped it, then the drawing, into the leather pouch at his hip. "It will be safe there." He tapped the pouch nervously. Abruptly he stood up. "Come on. I have something to show you. Something too big to fit in here."

"Where are we going? I don't know if I should…"

"I just want to show you my home. That's all."

"Oh." Twig imagined a little cave, perhaps tucked away along the coastline. Was it warm and cozy or damp and gloomy? Maybe it wasn't a cave at all, but a treehouse! High up in the cedars, safe from the wild unicorns.

She followed him around the rocks, over a pile of driftwood, and into the lichen-draped trees. Under her bare feet, the sand gave way to dirt.

Ben paused a few yards into the woods and picked up his quiver and bow, which he'd left tucked between some tree roots.

There was a flutter of green in the air, brighter than the evergreens surrounding them. "Mr. Murley's bird!" It swooped right toward them.

Ben smiled and held out his arm and made a cooing noise. "*My* bird. Emmie."

The bird perched on Ben's arm and made expectant pecking motions at his sleeve. Ben took a pinch of seeds from his pocket and held them out.

"Open your hand." He dropped the seeds into Twig's palm, and the bird leaned toward it, but it still clung to Ben's sleeve. "Hold it closer. Next time she'll go to you, I think."

"Is she some kind of parrot?" Twig admired the emerald-green plumage and the amber-colored beak pecking the seeds out of her hand.

"She's a letter pigeon. Look at her leg."

Twig examined the tiny leather tube attached to one of the pigeon's legs.

"She's the most beautiful pigeon I've ever seen. How many creatures do you have?"

"Just her and Indy."

"Where *is* Indy?"

"You'll see."

Ben pulled his cloak around him and strode deeper into the trees, Emmie riding on his shoulder. Twig stumbled after him, head down, seeking the softest places to set her bare feet.

When Ben stopped, she almost bumped right into his back. Twig looked up, and there was Indy. The unicorn stallion shook his head and snorted softly. His ears were flattened. One ear turned at their approach, but the other he tuned straight ahead, at a strangely thick wall of fog. A shroud wrapped around the trees in the middle of the island.

The sun was warm on Twig's back, but seeing that

net of misty white just a few paces away made goose bumps rise along her skin. The frightening fog of her first moments on Lonehorn Island had hidden in the woods, waiting to creep out over the rest of the island again—or for Twig to wander in.

Ben said hello to Indy. Then, with Emmie the pigeon still perched on his shoulder, he stepped into the mist. It folded around him, swallowing him whole.

"Ben!" Without thinking, Twig lunged after him.

Ben's misty form paused. "You cannot tell anyone about this."

Twig's heart pounded. The moist wind whistled in her ears, *You don't belong here, Twig. Get out. Get out while you can.*

Twig just nodded at Ben. What would she say, anyway? *I know where the mist hides, even when the sun comes out? I know where to find the island's secrets?* Twig hugged herself tight. Hadn't enough of the island's secrets found her already? She didn't need any more to keep.

"Twig!" A real voice this time, solid and familiar, piercing the fog with a hint of out-of-place sunshine.

It was Janessa, somewhere in the woods nearby, looking for her.

"I have to go, Ben."

"I need your help," Ben blurted. "Please. Don't go."

Twig glanced over her shoulder. She knew Ben was the kind of boy who wasn't used to asking, let alone begging. The word *please* sounded like it almost got stuck on the way out. She didn't want to say no, but how could she say yes to moving even one step farther into that strange, swirling chill? Why did she need to be here with him? How could *she* help?

But Ben took her hand, and her feet moved forward, after his, into the whispering veil. She shook off a shudder and tried to tell herself there was nothing strange going on. This was just a spot where the fog collected, and Ben was just a lonely boy.

A few moments later, Ben stopped again. He let go of Twig's hand and glanced back at her.

"This is where you live?" she asked.

Ben gestured at a cluster of hemlocks whose branches swept through the curtain of mist, to the forest floor.

"In there. Through there."

Ben pushed the evergreen branches open and stood aside for Twig. Emmie flew in first, her vibrant plumage becoming a dull blur in the cloudlike air. Twig entered the shadows of the branches after the bird. Those shadows were so deep, too dark for day. Lightened only by the misty white that hung in the air, thicker than ever. Twig stumbled backward and the boughs snagged at her hair. Ben caught her wrist, steadying her.

She emerged on the other side of the trees. Now she stood in the center of a ring of low-growing hemlocks clustered near the base of the massive, fluted trunk of a much older red cedar. No signs of a treehouse. Nothing that said *home*.

Emmie darted past. A breeze wafted through the mist, smelling musty, yet nothing like Lonehorn Island, or western Washington even. Nothing like the world Twig knew.

Emmie cooed. Far away, another pigeon returned her cry. Twig looked up just in time to see Emmie disappear into the lichen-draped branches of the red cedar. A flash of light illuminated a little circle of the mist, and for an instant, Emmie glittered jewel green.

Then the light was gone, and an eerie breeze, stirring up the mist rather than clearing it away, made the only sound, a faint swishing—until the branches snapped down behind Twig, locking her in.

CHAPTER 22

T WIG PIVOTED AROUND, HER throat closing. Ben's grip tightened on her hand, but he seemed unconcerned. He was Ghost Boy again, blending into the mysterious fog as if he were a part of it.

Twig almost pulled away. Almost ran.

"Where are we?" she managed to ask.

"Near the entrance to Silverforest in Westland—Terracornus."

"Terracornus?"

"Sometimes one world bumps up against another, and people find a passage between them. This is one of those passages. I wish this one had been forgotten like the original passage from England to Terracornus. All I can do is keep the door locked." Ben's expression darkened. "Unfortunately, I'm not the only one with a key, and only the queen can change the locks."

"Door? What queen? The Queen of England?"

"The Queen of Westland. People first came to Terracornus from England. That's why we speak English. But they're a different people now. And yes, there is a door in here. Unicorns go through it whenever someone lets them."

"This isn't funny, Ben. I don't like these kinds of stories."

"No, it isn't funny. Dagger's healed. He's hunting again. The others were foraging, but now they're back to following Dagger's lead—back to being predators. You have to believe. You know there's more to this island, Twig."

Ben reached under his shirt and pulled something out—a key. He approached the huge red cedar trunk.

Did Ben expect her to believe the tree was a magic door? That they were going to walk right through it? Twig scrutinized the rough bark in the semidarkness. She couldn't make out any seams.

She waited for Ben to mutter a spell, but he just slid the key right into the bark. Twig put her hand to the trunk where the key had gone in. The keyhole had been invisible in the shadows and the mist.

The key turned with a click, and Ben pulled the door

open a crack. Thicker mist snaked through the crevice, finding Twig and wrapping her in its strange scent. Ben slid his fingers around the door and began to open it wider.

"No!" Twig choked. "That's enough."

Ben pushed the door shut. The lock clicked.

"Is that where Wild Light came from? Is that where you want to send her?" Twig shook at the thought. But if Wild Light wasn't safe here on the island…

"She cannot go back. Terracornus isn't safe anymore. Now all the unicorns of Westland belong to the queen. She wants them for the war with Eastland. She'll take Wild Light or any unicorn she can get her hands on. There are only a few wild unicorns left in Terracornus, lonely, herdless, hiding. But the queen's rangers are always hunting for them."

"They kill them?" Twig's hands clenched into fists.

"They round them up and train them for battle. Many of them die in training. More die in the war itself. The unicorns of Lonehorn Island are the last free herd."

"In the real—in my world, a long time ago, armies used horses. A lot of them died."

"They never used horses like the Terracornians use

unicorns. In Terracornus, unicorns *are* the weapons. Horses never died here the way unicorns die there."

"But here, Dagger and the others'll come after her to try to make her join their herd?"

Ben shook his head. "They'll come after her to *kill* her. Wild Light is Indy's daughter. They know that by her scent. Dagger sees Indy as a rival. Wild unicorns kill their rivals and their offspring."

"What about Indy? You left him out there!"

"They hunt at night and stay hidden during the day. Besides, he can smell them coming and let me know if he needs my help."

"You could've brought him with us."

"I don't bring him here unless I have to. He doesn't like it. It's too close to Terracornus. He wants to stay here in the Earth Land. All unicorns do once they're here. One whiff of Lonehorn Island air, and they remember the Earth Land is the world they were really made for, where they belong."

"Ter—Terracornus isn't where the unicorns come from?"

"It's where emerald pigeons are from. That's why Emmie's always more than willing to go. But the unicorns—they were taken there. When Terracornus was found, it was mostly empty, and they were sent to live in it, to keep them safe from humans."

"But Wild Light is here, on the island, and she isn't safe." Twig swallowed hard.

Ben nodded. "The herd will come after her. It's only a matter of time."

"Twig!" The voice was so faint, muffled by branches and by fog, at first she thought she'd imagined it. "Twig!" It was Regina this time.

She broke away and ran back the way she'd come. Ben darted ahead, and for a moment Twig thought he was going to block her way, but he held the low hemlock boughs open for her instead.

"I need your help to make this island safe again. For Wild Light. For everyone."

"I have to go!"

She ran through the mist, and she didn't look back. All Twig wanted was to feel the sun on her cheeks, to see the girls and the Murleys, to go home and throw her arms around Wild Light's neck—to forget about Lonehorn Island's secrets.

"I found her!" Regina said as soon as Twig burst into view.

Twig grabbed Regina's sleeve and pulled her toward the beach. They were still dangerously close to Ben and Indy, to the strange fog.

In the distance, Mandy called, "Regina found her!"

Girls came running from both directions of the beach, sand and water flying at their heels.

"Oh, good," Mrs. Murley said. "We haven't lost our Twig after all."

Mr. Murley counted the girls. "Six girls. All set to go?"

Casey and Mandy picked up their backpacks and brushed the sand off. Janessa took a sandy shoe in each hand and clapped them together, and Mandy shrieked that Janessa had gotten sand in her eye and threw her own shoe at Janessa, and Taylor made them both apologize and everyone forgot to ask Twig where she'd been.

Casey reached for Twig's hand and smiled. It was just an afternoon at the beach, and Casey was enjoying it. Twig was glad for her, glad to be here with the Murleys and the girls, laughing and bickering and singing their way back to the path.

But Twig couldn't help feeling strange being with

them, being normal—not just because she was Twig, but because she was the only one who knew the secrets at the heart of Lonehorn Island.

CHAPTER 23

THAT EVENING, TWIG CALLED Rain Cloud in from the pasture first, to give Wild Light a little more time to dance, and to give herself a few minutes alone to watch her after she took care of Rain Cloud.

Twig was leaning against the pasture fence, laughing at Wild Light's antics and trying not to think about the sort of cruel creatures who'd like to put an end to them, when the unicorn stopped her leaping and sniffed. She perked her ears toward the woods and gave her *hello* nicker.

Twig jogged to the fence, toward the shadow she knew was Ben. Wild Light bounded after her, and Twig hurriedly took hold of her halter, for she seemed about to let her enthusiasm propel her right out of the pasture and into the woods.

"Hello there, Wild Light," Ben whispered from the other

side of the fence. "Calm down now before you get us all in trouble."

"She's so determined to get to you. What are we going to do if she figures out how to jump the fence?"

"Another reason why I need you, Twig."

Twig didn't answer.

"A friend of mine is coming to visit me tonight in the hemlock circle."

The circle in the heart of the mist. The shadowy ring Twig never wanted to enter again.

"What kind of friend?"

"A great herder named Merrill. He worked with my father. I sent Emmie with a message for him to meet me."

"Herders, Terracornus, passages—Ben, I just can't—"

"You cannot believe it? Even after what you've seen?"

Twig's shoulders sagged. "I don't want to."

"You don't have a choice!" Ben reached for her arm. His expression softened. "I have a plan. A way we can work things out. I know it must seem strange. My father told me a bit about the Earth Land. It was hard to imagine the things he described, even that—truck?—they keep on the ranch."

Twig nodded.

"I don't understand how it works," Ben said.

"I guess I don't really understand how those things work either."

"But you know they're real."

Twig twisted her boot in the grass. She couldn't deny it.

"Just listen, and I'll try to explain. Everyone in Terracornus used to be a herder. Long ago, unicorns were hunted in the Earth Land, until there were only a few left. Their horns were very valuable, thought to be magic."

Twig cringed. No wonder Ben had been so irritated by her calling them magic.

"When the passage was discovered, from England to Terracornus, those who knew better rounded up the last of the unicorns and herded them into that new, empty land, where they would be safe. The herders watched over them, and when their numbers increased, they separated one herd from another, so they wouldn't fight and kill each other off. That was hundreds of years ago. Things are different now. Terracornians have forgotten their plan to return the unicorns to the Earth Land. Most of them have forgotten the Earth Land altogether. And this world has moved on without them."

Twig rubbed a strand of hair between her thumb and forefinger. "And your friend, the one you want me to meet, he's from Terracornus?"

"That's right."

"Maybe he can help you send them back! What are they doing on Lonehorn Island anyway? Who let them through that door?"

"My father believed a herder who wanted to reintroduce unicorns to this world brought the first few here. Instead of just watching over the island, protecting the passage from being discovered, Lonehorn Island's herders watched over the island's herd too. We cannot send them back, Twig. They'll all die if we do. Unicorns as they're meant to be will die."

"But with Dagger as their leader, they're not what they're meant to be anyway, are they?"

"Merrill can help me fix that, but he's going to need convincing. Seeing you—seeing what's at risk here on the island—might persuade him to come. I told him about you in my message."

"Oh. Well…" Twig glanced over her shoulder at the house and the stable. Wild Light nudged her. Twig took her muzzle in her hands and stroked it and looked into her silvery eyes—wild but filled with love. That herd had once been like her. "I'll come. Just tell me when."

"A couple hours before sunrise."

In the dark. She'd just agreed to enter that strange, clinging fog in the dark.

• • •

Twig threw her covers back. She slid her bare feet onto the purple throw rug between her bed and Casey's. She sat there for a moment, listening, trying to detect any howls through the walls, through the woods. What if tonight they woke and went on the hunt?

She should just get back in bed, forget about this craziness. Even if nothing happened out there, if she got caught...

A shuddery breath escaped Casey, the kind that found its way out no matter how you tried, no matter how you didn't want somebody to hear. Twig knew what it was to be little and alone and to cry herself to sleep.

She tiptoed to Casey's bed and put a tentative hand on

her hair. Casey wiggled closer, and Twig pulled her the rest of the way into her lap.

"It's okay now. You're here now. Whatever happened before, that stuff doesn't happen here."

Then the tears sprang up in Twig's eyes too, because she knew that it was true—that whatever was waiting and hunting in the woods around them, whatever was threatening to undo what the Murleys were trying to do, she was safe here, in these walls. The Murleys were for real, and the girls were liars and thieves and sulkers and impossible arguers and tantrum throwers, but they were for real too. And she was about to slip out of here, away from them, and maybe get herself hurt or killed and ruin it all. Forever.

She couldn't stay here forever anyway, she reasoned. It couldn't last forever. And if she didn't go, how long would it be safe here for anyone?

"Casey, I have to go somewhere for a little while."

Casey pushed herself up onto her elbow. "Where?"

"Here, on the island, sort of. It has to do with the wild boy. But I'll be back."

"How long are you gonna be gone?"

"I'll be back before chores. Don't worry."

Twig tucked Casey's doll under her arm. She got dressed and made her bed. She'd sneaked her boots and jacket into her room earlier. She slid her backpack out from under her pillow and put it on and wriggled her feet into her boots.

Casey was still awake, watching. Twig paused, then shrugged her backpack off and took out her drawing of Wild Light, horn and all—the one she'd kept for herself. She'd decided to play it safe and send Daddy the one without the horn. She tiptoed to Casey's bed and held it out to her.

"It's only for you, okay? Don't let anyone else see it."

"Okay." Casey unfolded the drawing and held it up to the moonlight. She stared at it for a moment, then lowered the paper. "Is it for real?"

Twig just smiled. "I have to go."

"Twig?"

"Yeah?"

"Come back."

"I will."

CHAPTER 24

BEN WAS WAITING FOR Twig behind the pasture shelter. He gave her a nod and hurdled the fence. Twig clambered after him, then stopped in the shadow of the tree line. It was so dark.

"I have a flashlight," she offered.

Ben looked confused. "Flush light?"

"Flashlight. You know, you hold it in your hand and push the button, and it lights up."

"No light."

Then he grabbed her hand and pulled her into the deepening darkness of the woods. "Indy's in the hollow," he whispered.

Twig gripped his hand tight. It was still night-dark, and it would be darker the farther they ventured into the trees, where the wild unicorns might be waiting.

Ben wove deftly into the woods, holding a branch back for her now and then. Twig tried to duck when he ducked, to step where he stepped, but she kept miscalculating, hitting her shin on a log, lurching down into a hole. Her stomach grew more fluttery and anxious each time she tripped, her steps more flustered and fumbling.

"How can you see?"

"I don't need to see much here because I know the path."

"There's a path?"

"Not just one path. I try to vary which way I go so I don't wear things down too much, and make it obvious that someone comes through here. But I know the routes from the pasture to the hollow."

Indy greeted them with a soft nicker before Twig even realized they were about to enter the hollow. Just a few more steps, and there they were, free of the underbrush, in the flat area beneath the trees.

"He always stays for you, doesn't he?"

"I had to train him to. It's not safe to tie him up."

"If you tie him," Twig said, holding back a shudder, "and they come after him, he can't escape."

"That's right."

Indy gave Ben an expectant look, and Ben took an apple from his pouch. The unicorn ate it with a crunch of satisfaction, but still with a wary ear turned toward the forest.

"There's another apple in my pouch." Ben rubbed Indy's neck. "Get it out and feed it to him."

"Me?"

"He's got to like you if you're to ride him."

"I'm going to ride him?"

"With me of course. The more you dither about it," he said in a confident, soothing tone meant to keep Indy at ease, "the more convincing we'll have to do, and we don't have much time."

Twig held the apple tentatively out to Indy. She couldn't help recalling Ben's words: *He was the fiercest, the wildest.*

"See there, boy? She's a friend. She's going to ride with me, just for a little while."

"That's right, Indy," Twig added in the smoothest manner she could manage. "There's not much to me at all. You'll see."

"There is more to you than you think, Twig."

Heat rushed over Twig's face.

Ben mounted Indy and offered her a hand up. Twig

climbed up behind him, and Indy let out a snort of protest, but it sounded more obligatory than angry. Twig slid
her arms around Ben's waist. She'd never ridden anything
other than a pony, let alone a unicorn, and she'd never
been quite so close to Ben.

Ben said, "Hang on tighter," to Twig, and, "Yah!" to Indy.

He leaned into Indy's neck, and the forest sped by in a
black-green blur. Twig held on as tight as she could. She
marveled at the unicorn's nimbleness in dark, thick woods
that Rain Cloud would have picked his way complainingly,
ploddingly through.

Twig squeezed her eyes shut, and she felt Indy's power
and speed. She pressed her forehead against Ben's back. His
cloak was softer than she'd expected, his heartbeat faster.
She couldn't tell whether Ben's heart was racing with anticipation or with plain old fear. Strange things were happening. Stranger things were going to happen. And she was
riding a unicorn in the purple-black before dawn to a passage that led into another world. To convince a man from
that world to save everything she loved about her own.

Chapter 25

TWIG TUCKED HER CHIN into the collar of her shell as she took her first breath of the strange, damp haze. Indy neighed his protest, but he inched forward.

"Just to the hemlocks, boy. Not through the passage. I promise."

Ben had told Twig a little about this friend they were going to see. Merrill had been his father's right-hand man before Ben stepped into the role, before the two of them were left to handle the guardianship of Lonehorn Island on their own. Twig didn't understand how that had happened, and Ben was very tight-lipped about it. It had something to do with the Queen of Westland. That was all she could figure out.

They left Indy at the edge of the cluster of hemlocks. The branches swished down behind her, and Twig blinked. Instead of black shadows, a yellow-orange light suffused the fog inside the hemlock circle. There was a crackle, and the light danced higher. A dark shadow rose out of the mist, a tall form that seemed to wobble much like the muted, dancing light.

"Merrill!" Ben called.

The shadow took form as it drew near. Merrill's smile was lopsided but genuine. He held a weathered hand up in greeting. A dark green woolen cap fitted his head with a snugness that suggested his hair was either very close-cropped or gone entirely. A thin, white scar cut through the gray-black stubble on his cheeks and chin, and he stepped forward with a lurch that drew Twig's attention to the odd fit of his pant leg. Though there was a boot on his left foot, Twig suspected the foot was artificial. Merrill's life as a herder had apparently not been gentle, yet there was gentleness in his gaze—a bright, steady gaze that made it easy for Twig to imagine he'd once carried himself with a similarly steady stride.

Ben threw his arms around Merrill with uncharacteristic abandon.

Merrill squeezed him, then ran a big hand over Ben's head. "It's been too long, boy."

"I know it."

Merrill released Ben and took a step back. He looked him over, then gave him a nod of approval and turned to Twig. Twig swallowed and willed herself not to look down at her boots.

"And this is your friend Twig?" the old herder's accent was much stronger than Ben's. It made each word seem powerful and strange to Twig.

"Yes, sir." Twig didn't know where the *sir* came from; it just seemed the proper way to address a man like Merrill.

Merrill shook her hand. "Well, come over to the fire, little one, where it's warm."

Twig followed him toward the flickering light. A campfire! What a relief to enter the circle of light and smoke that defied the otherworldly mist.

A rough woolen blanket was spread on the earth before the fire. Merrill carefully lowered himself, sticking his artificial leg straight out and bending the other one in. Twig sat next to Ben, across from Merrill.

"I got word that you needed my help, Ben-boy. You made no mention of your father, and now here you are without him. Where is he? Has something happened?"

Ben pulled his knees up to his chest. "Gone."

"Gone?" Merrill took off his hat. His hand was shaking. "Darian, gone?"

When Merrill let his own tears fall, Twig felt like crying too. In her head, she said *Darian* over and over. It was the first she'd heard Ben's father's name. It sounded so noble and strong, especially the way Merrill said it.

"It was Dagger. He attacked, and Father was wounded fighting him off. He died the next day."

Merrill sniffed loudly. "And Dagger is still out there, still a threat. Your message was clear enough about that."

"That's right."

"What now then, boy? What are you trying to do?"

"What my father would have me do."

"Are you now, Ben? You think he'd want you going after Dagger?"

"There are people on the island, Merrill. Good people. Girls like her."

"Littler ones too," Twig added.

"We need the herders' help, not just to keep Dagger from poisoning the herd forever, but also to protect those girls."

"The herders have been disbanded. You know that."

"You can get them together again. They'll listen to you."

"Not against the queen's wishes, they won't. Not anymore."

"We only need a few. Just—"

Merrill slapped his hat against his artificial leg. "Not anymore, I said! Listen to me. You let this alone."

"They're the last free herd! How can I leave them to what they're becoming? Killers of each other, of innocent horses, of people! How can I stand by and let them attack Island Ranch again?"

"The queen has already banished a good number of us to the Barrenlands. The ones who wouldn't listen. The next one will be tried for treason."

"Treason? For doing your job? The work our ancestors went to Terracornus to do?"

"It's not our job anymore. Not yours either, Ben of the Island. I'm sorry. I've got no desire to spend the rest of my years fighting the bitter cold and a bunch of bitterer herders for a spot by a meager coal fire, let alone to hang from a noose in the castle square."

"That's it, then, Merrill?"

"Take this girl back to her people, Ben-boy, and come stay with me. Any son of Darian is welcome in my home."

"Any son?" Ben said sharply.

Merrill gave him a hard look. "Any son. But you've known me long enough to know you'd be welcome either way, boy."

"I thank you, Merrill. And I'm sure my father would too. But we both know he'd thank you more if you helped me do what I need to do."

"It seems we disagree," said Merrill, sliding his hands into his pockets, "about just what it is you need to do."

"It seems so. Thanks anyway." Ben tightened his cloak and rose, stepping back into the swirling mist. "Come on, Twig."

Numbly, Twig followed Ben. With Twig riding behind him, Ben sent Indy cutting through the web of mist and trees at a near gallop.

Outside the shrouded circle, the morning glared shockingly bright. What time was it? What was she going to say to the Murleys? She'd be in trouble for sure, and Merrill had been no help. It was all for nothing.

"What now?" she asked.

"Nothing now!"

Twig held on stiffly to Ben's back, trying to resist the alternating urges to shove him off or to hug him tight and cry in shared frustration.

Twig let go of Ben, reached around, and grabbed at the reins. "Stop!"

"What are you doing?"

Twig jumped down, hands on her hips. Ben glared at her.

"You can't just give up. You can't hold them off forever. If they attack, how many can you shoot before the rest of them are all over you?"

"I'm not giving up! But I'm one rider and Indy is one tame unicorn. That's all I have."

"You'll have two tame unicorns once Wild Light is grown."

Indy pawed impatiently at the ground.

"And what about a rider?" Ben said quietly. His eyes searched Twig's.

Twig felt her mouth fall partway open. "I'm no rider," she said hoarsely. She'd never ridden Wild Light. No saddle had ever touched her perfect white back. She was too young for that. But the thought of attempting that when Wild Light was bigger, wilder…she grew more unruly every day.

"No," Ben said. "You're not. Not until you claim her."

"I can't ride a unicorn! I'm a scrawny girl who's only been riding a tame pony for a few months. And you expect me to get Wild Light to let me ride her? And what if she did? Then what? I'd teach her how to fight off a whole herd of unicorns who are trying to kill her?"

Twig laughed a high, humorless laugh, and a part of her felt terrible at the sound of it, but the anger at Ben's expectations was just as strong.

Ben's brown eyes gleamed with intensity. "A rider doesn't teach her unicorn *how* to fight; she shows her *when* to fight. And if her heart is right, she gives her unicorn the right reason to do it. As for Indy and Wild Light, the bows and swords of riders can help protect them against the greater numbers of the herd. And if I can hold them off until you and Wild Light have some training…"

"Ben—"

"I'll help you."

He looked so sure. How could he be so certain? "If I say yes—*if* I say yes—what exactly are you asking me to do?"

"I want to turn them back. It will probably take killing Dagger to do that, but I'm trying to save them just as much as I'm trying to protect the people on this island. They are the last free herd after all."

Twig blinked at him. It was crazy to think of her, Twig Tupper, riding her very own unicorn and helping steer a herd of the wildest and rarest creatures back the way they belonged. There had to be something else, some other way. Ben's plan was not going to work. Wild Light wouldn't even be mature enough to ride for months. They'd never make it that long alone.

Twig tipped her chin back up. "Take me back to Merrill."

CHAPTER 26

TWIG TUMBLED OFF INDY'S back in her haste, and
Merrill's strong hands grasped her under the arm-
pits, pulled her away from Indy's hooves, and set her on
her feet.

"Whoa, there. What's going on here? You trying to get
yourself killed, little one?"

"No, Ben's the one who's going to get himself
killed if you won't help! Can't you see that? Because he
won't—he—" A sob escaped. "He won't give up on us.
Ben won't give up on what his father wanted, on those
unicorns, on us girls who everybody else gave up on.
That's why he understands that the girls won't give up
on the ranch and the Murleys won't give up on them."
She turned to Ben. "And neither will I. Even if your idea
of me riding Wild Light is stupid and crazy."

Ben steadied Indy and dismounted. He didn't say anything, but he reached for Twig and pulled her into a sideways hug.

"You, little one, riding Wild Light?" Merrill said. "Wind Catcher's filly?"

Twig felt the heat of embarrassment under hotter tears. Stupid, stupid Twig. What was she thinking?

But Merrill said, "Could be this boy's not so stupid as you think, Twig-girl. Could be this old man was the stupid one. You helped me understand a thing or two myself, I think. If you're willing to learn, then I'm willing to risk my hide to keep you and that ranch safe long enough to do it."

"You are?" Ben said.

"The filly trusts her?"

"More than anyone. She even lets Twig halter her and lead her."

"Sounds like you've got a unicorn," Merrill said to Twig. "That filly may not know it, but she's chosen you to be her rider. Doubt she'd let anyone else take that role now."

"What do you mean," Twig said between sniffs, "'chosen'?"

"When unicorns were hunted, they learned to fear men, and they passed that fear and hostility on, generation after generation. When men first tried to manage unicorns, it was clear we'd need to learn to ride a few of them, and those few would need to trust us. What can you herd a unicorn with but another unicorn? What other creature could keep up and defend itself? It seemed an impossible task, but those first herders discovered something about unicorns. Sometimes they'll choose a human to trust. One who respects their intelligence, their independence, and who gives them a sense of purpose. They'll work with that person, let her ride. And when a unicorn bonds with a rider, it's like healing an ancient wound."

"She'll need a sword and a bow," Ben said. "She can practice on her own until Wild Light is big enough to ride."

"A sword and a bow?" Twig said.

"That can be arranged," Merrill said. "We'll teach you to fight, to ride, and eventually to herd."

"A maiden," Ben said with a smirk, "to tame the wild unicorns."

•••

A pale sun was rising when Ben left Indy in the hollow and slipped through the trees with Twig. Twig could hear the truck's engine as they made their way through the underbrush just outside Island Ranch. Frantic voices called her name.

"Oh no." She hesitated at the edge of the fence. "That's not good." She'd managed to come back in one piece, but too late.

"Hey." Ben caught her sleeve. "Are you going to be all right?"

"Take Indy and find somewhere good to hide. There might be people all over the island looking for me."

Why hadn't she thought of that before? The Murleys weren't Mom. Of course they'd notice she was gone. When they couldn't find her, they'd do the responsible thing—call for help, have the authorities search the island. And then what would they find? What if they'd already found the herd?

CHAPTER 27

TWIG RAN FOR THE house. The sooner she got back, the sooner they'd stop searching the island. The truck was crunching along the gravel driveway when Twig came sprinting across the pasture.

Mandy met her at the pasture gate. "You're in *big* trouble."

Twig didn't stop running until she got closer to the house, and Mr. Murley slammed the truck door shut behind him and came running up to her. Mrs. Murley came out and stood on the front porch and just stared at her.

"Twig," Mr. Murley said, "where have you been?" His face was creased with worry, and Mrs. Murley's eyes were wet with tears.

"I'm sorry. I'm really sorry." She wanted to say that it wouldn't happen again; she hated that the truth was just the opposite. She'd agreed to meet with Ben and Merrill again in the hemlock circle.

"Twig," Mrs. Murley said in a cracked, quiet voice, "we had to call your stepmother—before we called the police."

"You called the police?"

"Not yet, thank God. I just called her to tell her I was contacting the Sheriff's Department." Mrs. Murley hugged her arms around herself, and Twig wished she would hug her instead.

The other girls trickled toward the porch from all corners of the property. They murmured and shushed each other. Twig looked at her boots and wished she'd never come back.

Mr. Murley put his arm around her. He gave her a slow, firm hug, but then he pulled back. "Do you have any idea the things a parent imagines when a child just vanishes on an island?"

Twig was about to remind him that Keely wasn't her parent, when she realized that Mr. Murley was talking just as much about himself and Mrs. Murley. Had they thought she'd fallen and hit her head on the rocks? Wandered into the woods and got her leg caught on a tree root and broken it? Clambered out in the tide pools and gotten smashed by a rogue wave and swept out to sea, never to be seen again?

Mr. Murley's cell phone rang. "It's your stepmother." He turned it on. "Hello, Mrs. Tupper. We have good news. Yes, she's turned up. Well, we're just sitting down to talk about it. She just—yes, of course. Sure. I'll be there… just a minute."

Mr. Murley covered the speaker with his hand. "She wants to talk to you, Twig."

"Is she coming here?"

"Well, yes. She's on her way. She was ready to help with a search and rescue operation."

"But I'm back, and I'm fine. She can go back home now."

"Twig, I don't think you realize how serious this is. You were *missing*. She wants to see you and she wants to… check on things."

Twig's jaw tensed. She reached out her hand and Mr. Murley put the phone in it. "Keely?"

"Twig!"

"I don't want you coming here and I don't have anything else to say!"

Twig pressed the red button, tossed the phone back to

Mr. Murley, and spun around. She waited for Mr. Murley to grab her arm and yank her back, for Mrs. Murley to say something, but no one moved, except to fumble for the phone.

She went to the stable to see Wild Light and to see if Rain Cloud needed anything too. She cleaned some stray bedding out of Rain Cloud's water bucket and refilled it with fresh water. When she apologized for missing breakfast, Rain Cloud gave her a disapproving glare that made Twig want to cry.

She left Rain Cloud and went to Wild Light and whispered the whole story into her ears. Wild Light nuzzled against Twig and told her that she understood.

Janessa came to the stable to get Twig at lunchtime, but Twig said she wasn't hungry. She took her sketchbook and her ebony pencil out of her backpack and sketched Wild Light instead. She drew her beside Indy. Then she drew Ben riding Indy and herself riding Wild Light. Ben had his sword drawn. Twig shaded in a sword for herself too. She flipped over the page. She wanted to draw Dagger, but nothing she envisioned seemed quite right. The unicorns she drew were fierce but beautiful, light, graceful.

She couldn't picture a unicorn who matched the malicious sounds in the woods, the horrific story of Darian's death, or what she imagined had happened to Merrill's leg.

Casey's distinctive steps entered the stable, and Story's stall door creaked open. Twig put away her drawing materials and said good-bye to Wild Light.

She went to Story's stall. Casey sniffed, stroking her pony's nose. "I can't ride today. I don't know when they'll let me ride again."

"Why?" Twig said meekly.

"'Cause I told them you were in the bathroom. That you were sick. Not to bother you because you were embarrassed."

"What!"

"I told them you had the poops. It worked too, until breakfast!"

"I didn't expect you to *lie* like that."

"Well, what did you expect me to do, then?"

"I don't know." Twig picked a strand of stray hair out of Casey's puffy eyes.

"I told them I knew you were okay, but they wouldn't believe me 'cause I couldn't tell them why."

"I'm sorry." Twig slipped her arm around Casey's

shoulders. "But—the poops?" Under her arm, Casey's shoulders shook with a little laugh. Twig laughed too. "I wish I could tell you all about it, but I made a promise not to, you know?"

"A promise to the wild boy?"

Twig didn't answer. Maybe she'd ask Ben if she could tell Casey, but not now. Not before they had things figured out. Casey didn't need to know how bad it was.

Another familiar pair of boot steps approached. Twig inched out of the stall and stuffed her hands in her jacket pockets and stared up at Mrs. Murley. Mrs. Murley looked even more troubled than she had before.

"Twig," she said, "your stepmother is here."

CHAPTER 28

MRS. MURLEY LED TWIG to the office.

Keely rose from the office couch as soon as she saw Twig. "I got hold of your dad. He's concerned, and—"

"I'm happy here," Twig blurted. "I'm me here. Doesn't that count for anything?" Daddy knew? He'd make Keely take her home for sure!

"Twig, you just disappeared! You were gone all morning, and you won't tell anyone where you went or why. It's clear you aren't making much progress here. I mean, you did your schoolwork this spring and that's good, but you haven't even spoken about what happened. Before you came here, I mean. It's important to talk about things if you're going to get better. And you haven't even mentioned…Twig, sweetie, maybe you need a professional with a different approach."

"You're going to send me somewhere else? Just because you don't want me doesn't mean nobody else does. People want me, Keely. People want me here!"

As soon as she said it, Twig throbbed with the fear that it wasn't true. What if the Murleys didn't want her anymore after what she'd done? She'd just broken their trust, and she couldn't even offer them an explanation, and now Keely was reminding them why she'd been sent here in the first place.

"This isn't about you not being wanted, for Chr—for heaven's sake. We want you to get better so you can come home. But if you're still a danger to other children…"

There was an awful silence. Twig squeezed her eyes shut and tried not to remember the thud of Emily's body on the hood of the car. It had been the most awful sound Twig had ever heard, and Twig had heard a lot of awful things. But then the tires had screeched and the driver had screamed and Emily had bounced and landed with a horrible crunch on the road, and that had been worse.

Twig's mind rewound the memory, back to when she'd tried to stop Emily from riding that bike. "Wait!" she'd said. "Please!" Emily hadn't listened. Twig had run after her, down the hill, but it had been too late. Emily had picked up speed and picked up speed until she was hurtling down the hill. The wheel of her bike had flown off and so had Emily. And then the car had come, with terribly perfect timing.

Twig opened her eyes and met Mrs. Murley's grief-filled gaze. Grief for what Keely had told her Twig had done, or grief that Twig was going to have to leave? It was too much.

"I never hurt anybody!" Twig shouted at Keely. "I never would. Corey did that to Emily's bike, not me!"

Keely gasped. "Now you're going to try to blame Corey? Emily saw you with the tools, messing with her bike right before she got on it!"

"I was trying to fix it! I saw Corey doing something to it, and I was trying to fix it. He was mad at her for smashing his Lego tower to get back at him for—"

"Stop. Just stop with these lies."

Twig shook her head. "They are *not* lies." Corey hadn't even had to tell a lie in order for Keely to believe one. He'd sobbed and sobbed when Emily had gotten hurt, so hard he couldn't even talk. Keely and Emily had drawn their own conclusions, and Corey hadn't looked anyone in the eye from that moment until Twig left. Maybe he still hadn't.

It didn't matter much that Emily was all right now. She was only all right because she'd been wearing one of those helmets Keely insisted on and that Twig always forgot to put on.

"Corey didn't think something like that would happen. He felt terrible. He would've fessed up if you'd ever bothered to ask him. But you wanted to think it was me. You wanted me to be as bad as you thought I was. Well, I don't care what you think of me, but this is my home now. Just leave me here, and leave me alone!"

There was a long silence. "Twig," Mr. Murley finally said, "why don't you go wait in your room for a few minutes while we talk?"

Twig gave Keely a good glare before she went.

She climbed into bed and pulled the grass-green covers over her head. The suitcase was in the closet. She pictured herself having to pull it out and fill it with her things. She imagined it standing on the foot of her bed again like a tombstone. Her new life, over. Ben's plans, ruined. Wild Light, abandoned.

What if Keely believed her? Mrs. Murley did, she was sure of it. What if she convinced Keely? What excuse would Keely have to leave her here then? Oh, she'd messed everything up. Just like she always did.

Twig flung the covers back and bolted upright. If she hurried, if she was quiet, maybe she could make it to the stable in time. Maybe—

"Twig?" Mrs. Murley knocked on the door.

"What?" Twig's voice was little more than a squeak.

"Come on out, honey, so we can all talk."

Twig wiped her sleeve across her eyes. She opened the door. Mrs. Murley handed her a tissue. The soft kind with scented lotion in it. She was going to miss those tissues. Twig blew her nose hard and Mrs. Murley hugged her harder.

"I don't know why you left, Twig, but I forgive you. I should've told you that right away. I'm sorry, honey."

Twig shook with a new sob. She was sorrier. Oh, she was so much sorrier.

Mrs. Murley swept Twig's hair out of her eyes, and Twig took a deep breath and gave them another wipe.

"Everyone's in the office."

Twig balled up the tissue in her fist and kept her arms

locked around Mrs. Murley's waist the whole way to the office, not caring one bit how she looked or what anyone thought. *I love you, Mrs. Murley. I love it here and I love you.* It was all she could think.

Keely was on the office couch, and Mr. Murley sat on the edge of the desk across from her, looking tired and holding a box of tissues in one hand. The wastebasket at the end of the desk was full of them.

"Twig." Keely wiped the last bit of her mascara, a black trickle, from the corner of her eye. "I believe you. I just spoke to Corey on the phone. He told me everything. He was afraid to say anything, afraid I'd send him away."

Twig let go of Mrs. Murley. She took a step backward, toward the door. Keely was going to take her away. Away from Wild Light. Away from Casey. Away from the Murleys and their prayers and their hugs and the bottomless pot of hot chocolate. She should've made a run for it while she had the chance. Maybe it wasn't too late.

"Twig." Mr. Murley slid off the desk and put a firm hand on her back. He knew what she was thinking. And now there was no way out of this. "Your stepmother wants you back."

Twig pulled away.

"But," he said, nudging her back toward him, "she wants what's best for you. We all do. She asked for my opinion, and I told her I think it would be good for you to stay here."

"Whatever you want, Twig," Keely said.

Twig dove at Mrs. Murley and threw her arms back around her. She'd been given a lot of hugs since she'd gotten here, but today was the first day Twig had given one to anyone who wasn't a pony—or a unicorn. She ran back to Mr. Murley and she hugged him too.

"This is what I want. I want to stay."

• • •

Ben adjusted the leather strap over Twig's shoulder, and Merrill took a step back. He gave her an appraising look, then smiled. Hand shaking, Twig gripped the leather-bound hilt and drew the short sword. It rung in the still, misty night, singing of a different world, making Keely and the hopelessness of last week seem so far away.

"It feels a little heavy now, but you'll get stronger," Merrill said.

Twig sheathed the sword, and Ben handed her the bow. "It was mine until last year. Father said I was ready for a bigger one, and he helped me make the one I use now."

"Who made this one?" Twig asked, trying to hold it as she'd seen Ben hold his.

"Darian," Merrill whispered. "A man of many talents."

Twig lowered the bow. "I shouldn't—I can't—maybe a different bow."

"This one's perfect for you," Merrill said. "You'll see."

Twig shook her head. "I don't deserve it."

"Neither did I." Ben's chin trembled. "It's a gift. You don't have to deserve it. You just have to use it the best you can."

• • •

After chores and a big Saturday breakfast, Twig gently lifted the bow out of her closet, where she'd hidden it. The smooth wood was worn smoother where Ben's hands had held it. How many hours had he practiced, starting when he was just a little boy? He'd learned to use it well, but could she, in so little time?

The door flung open and Casey rushed in.

"Twig, want to—wow!" She stopped, staring at the bow in Twig's hands, then the quiver of arrows at her feet.

Janessa ran in right behind Casey. "What *is* that?" she cried, loud enough to draw all the other girls in.

"Where did you get it?" Taylor said.

"Um…my closet," Twig said lamely.

Mr. Murley passed by the open door. Seeing the girls clustered around Twig, he paused and frowned. "What are you ladies up to in there?"

"Mr. M! Look what Twig's been hiding in that big old suitcase!" Janessa cried.

Twig's pulse raced. What was she going to say? What if they took it away because it was too dangerous? She should've kept it hidden. But she needed to practice in the daylight before she tried to use it in the dark. Though they were keeping her sword in the hollow for her, Ben and Merrill had insisted that she take the bow home and find a way to work with it.

The girls parted and let Mr. Murley through. His eyes widened, and he reached out to run his finger over the bow. "Incredible craftsmanship! It looks like something straight out of history. What kind of fiber is this bowstring made of?"

"I—I don't know," Twig said. "A friend gave it to me to use. I don't know how yet…but I'm going to learn." Twig lifted her chin, daring him to tell her she couldn't.

But Mr. Murley's eyes sparkled with interest. "Archery! I always wanted to practice archery. I'll make you a target, Twig—I've got some plywood in the shed—if you let me try my hand at it too."

Twig relaxed. "Deal," she said.

"I could do some research," Taylor said, "about technique, how to take care of it…"

All the girls began talking at once, clamoring to touch the bow.

"Hey!" Casey pushed in front of Twig, and they all stopped. "It's Twig's." Casey looked Twig right in the eye. At first she didn't say anything more. But her eyes said she knew this bow was special, that it hadn't been in her suitcase all this time. "Twig," she finally said, "it's the coolest thing I ever seen. None of us'll touch it, except Mr. Murley. We promise."

The girls nodded solemnly. Mandy scowled, but she said, "Promise."

Mr. Murley gave Casey a squeeze. "That's right. This isn't a toy. Fun as it is, it's a weapon. And a beautiful replica. We'll all help Twig, and she'll be handling it like a pro in no time."

If only Mr. Murley knew just what Twig had to handle. Learning to shoot an unmoving target in the daylight was one thing. Firing from the back of a leaping unicorn in the black of night was another.

November

CHAPTER 29

TWIG SLIPPED THROUGH THE night, head ducked against the pouring rain. The soggy earth sucked at her boots as she darted behind one of the pasture shelters. It was Friday, practice day.

Anxiously, Twig peered into the brush. Ben raised a hand to greet her, his cloaked figure barely visible on Indy's back. Relieved, Twig scrambled over. She didn't like to enter the woods alone, even after all this time, even though she knew the herd wouldn't be on the hunt tonight. She'd learned that wild unicorns' scents and moods changed with the seasons. Now that it was well into fall, the herd was much less active, saving their energy in a natural response to the colder weather and the scarceness of food. The instinct to go after their rivals kicked in only in the spring.

Twig climbed up behind Ben.

"Should we cancel when it rains like this, do you think?" Ben's words were muffled by his hood and an even more vigorous pelting of rain.

"It's fall. It's always raining. It'll be worse in winter."

"Unless it snows." Ben urged Indy on. His voice lifted with excitement. "I'm glad you came anyway. We have something new to show you."

"What is it?"

Had Merrill made a new dummy for her to slash at with the sword he'd given her from Terracornus? Her arms ached at the idea. She'd spent too many nights lifting that sword, swooshing and stabbing through mist and rain, hoping she'd never have to use it and, at the same time, praying she'd use it well if she did.

"You'll have to see it to believe it."

Indy bounded through the darkness and the driving rain. When he slowed down, Twig knew they were near the hollow. She looked up and saw Indy's horn extending, all on its own, as it did only when another unicorn was present. Twig went cold with fear. Without thinking, she reached for Ben's sword.

Ben put his hand over hers. "It's all right. You'll see."

"But they must be here!"

At the edge of the hollow, rain cascaded down the ever-green branches. Twig braced herself for a dousing, but Ben steered Indy through a gap between waterfalls, and then they were safe under the perfect umbrella of trees—where another unicorn was waiting, its horn fully extended in a deadly spiral.

Twig choked on a cry, then saw the rope around the creature's neck, tethering it to a tree, and Merrill standing nearby. The lantern hanging from a branch overhead cast a dim, bobbing light over the unicorn and the herder, il-luminating a slice of apple in his open palm.

Twig let out a breath. "You got one!"

She undid the Velcro at the collar of her shell and pushed her hood back to get a better look. It was a young stallion, a mottled gray-white, with a whiter mane. He bent his knees and ducked his head nervously, submissively to the side. Indy gave him a superior nicker, then turned away, accept-ing his desire for peace with an air of indifference.

Last Friday, Twig, Ben, and Merrill had been debating how to deal with the herd. They all agreed it would be ideal to track the herd, to go on the offensive during their months of winter lethargy, and try to eliminate Dagger before they started hunting again in the spring. If they all had unicorns to ride, Ben could take Dagger out with his bow, then join Twig and Merrill in herding the others. The problem was, they were two unicorns short.

Maybe now they were a step closer to being able to carry out that plan.

"We call him Marble. His coat looks like the stone. He wandered away from the others while they were asleep," Merrill explained. "I'm sure the trail of carrot pieces I dropped helped him wander farther than he would've."

"Too bad Dagger never wanders away from the others," said Twig.

"I know," Ben said. "But this one's been so easy."

"He does give us hope for the rest of the herd, though I've had a little help from the mixture of herbs I wrapped around those carrots. A little something to help keep him docile."

"Will you be able to ride him, Merrill?"

"In time, I hope. But it's too soon to try. He's still wild, still looking for the others."

Twig looked into the unicorn's eyes. "He doesn't look so wild to me. His eyes look kind of cloudy."

"That would be the concoction I fed him. Hate to do it, but we cannot have him calling out to the others, stirring them up. I'm hoping if we keep him away from them for a while, if he gets used to us and appreciates our tasty oats and apples, he'll calm down a bit on his own."

"That's going to take a long time, isn't it?"

"That filly was born in April by your calendar, right?" Merrill said.

"Right."

Merrill turned to Ben. "You've seen her. When do you think she'll be ready to ride?"

"February at the earliest. About three months from now."

"That just might be enough time for Twig to learn to ride her before spring comes in full force. We'll have to hope I have Marble's trust by then and that it's not too soon for Wild Light."

"Or too late for the rest of us," Twig said.

"None of that, now, Twig," Merrill said. "You've got training to do tonight, and quick, so you can slip back into bed before the sun rises."

Ben's eyes glittered with new excitement. "Tonight you're going to practice shooting while you ride."

"Indy?"

Ben nodded, and Twig gulped.

Though Ben kept him warm with blankets and, with Twig's help, well fed, Indy was less energetic than he had been in the warmer months. As Twig approached him, contemplating this impossible new task, she was glad he was a little slower, that he couldn't jump quite as high.

Twig began to pull herself up, but Indy neighed his refusal, and she backed away. The last thing she wanted was for Indy to move to the next phase. For a pony, that would mean showing his teeth. But Indy's horn was extended, and that's what he'd show her, with little jabbing motions meant to remind her he could run her right through.

"Whoa, boy," Ben said, "I'm coming too." He mounted and calmed Indy, then Twig joined him. "It will be different with Wild Light," he told Twig.

But what if it wasn't? What if the unicorns knew something Ben and Merrill refused to see—that she wasn't fit to ride?

Soon they were bounding out of the hollow and through the shadows and Twig was nocking arrows, trying to shoot at the tree trunks Merrill had marked with bands of white cloth whenever he said, "Now!" Her aim wasn't so bad, but she dropped every second arrow.

Twig's shell kept her warm, but she'd thrown off her hood in order to see better and her head was completely drenched. She tried to control her shivering, but it was so hard. She thought of the warm yellow house and the people she loved. She wanted to go back, and yet she wanted to keep trying, to do what she'd promised to do. Was this how Daddy felt when he went away for training, when he was deployed? The excitement mixed with the fatigue and the regret that it had to be done at all?

"All right. That's enough now, Twig-girl," Merrill said.

"It's a miserable night, and you've worked hard," Ben agreed.

Twig shook her head. "A few more minutes. One more time around."

This time, she dropped only two. She dismounted, and Merrill caught her cold, thin hand in his leathery one. "Well done. You're quite the archer."

"And soon you'll be a unicorn rider too," Ben said.

Twig smiled, but her stomach tightened. If Wild Light

refused her, it wouldn't matter how good an archer she was. It wouldn't matter that she was one of the ranch's strongest riders now. All this would be for nothing.

February

CHAPTER 30

A S SOON AS HER schoolwork was done, Twig put on her boots and grabbed her bow and quiver from the entryway. It was February, and as Twig headed for the pasture that now served as her bow range, she noticed that the crocuses were up in the flower beds around the porch, slim, green buds anxious for spring. Rather than a welcome reminder that glimpses of sunshine were just a couple months away, for Twig they were tiny warning flags, soon to unfurl.

Wild Light was nearly grown, almost as big as Indy, and Ben thought she was ready to ride. He wanted Twig to try tonight. The days of the unicorn wearing herself out bounding around the pasture and testing the ponies, then curling up, asleep in the pasture shelter, while Rain Cloud stood there looking after her were now few and far between.

More and more, Wild Light was separate from the ponies and Feather, searching and calling out to the woods, leaping, weaving, often with a sense of fierceness rather than playfulness. Sometimes she even seemed to charge at invisible opponents, tipping her head down, then up, to thrust with a horn that wasn't there—a horn that was supposed to be there.

Soon spring would be here, and the hungry howls would be back. Twig had to practice every chance she got. She took aim and shot. Her arrow hit its mark with a satisfying twang. But the real test, for her and for Wild Light, would come tonight.

• • •

Twig crept to the stable. Ben slipped out of the shadow of the eaves. There was no moonlight tonight, only darkness shrouded in mist. He gave her a nod. Ben believed she could do this. Who had believed she could do anything before she came to Lonehorn Island?

"I'll be right here," Ben said.

Twig nodded back, heart fluttering. She went into the

tack room and took down what she needed from the pegs on the wall, and then she went to Wild Light's stall. Wild Light stirred from her sleep. She smelled Twig and she nickered at her, in the way she only did at Twig.

"Wild Light," she said lovingly, "it's Twig. I know you want out. I know you want to run. You can run all over the island, but I have something to talk to you about first."

Twig willed her hand to stop trembling. It was no use. She squeezed her eyes shut and prayed for courage, for a courage Wild Light could feel.

What was she doing? This was stupid. No one was listening. Why would they? She was no unicorn rider. She was a worthless throwaway girl. She hadn't been able to keep her family together. She hadn't been enough for Daddy to stay or enough to make Mom happy. She hadn't managed to stop her mom from getting worse and worse. And then she'd done things for Mom. Stolen things. Helped her do things she knew she shouldn't. And all that time she'd been too big a coward to tell anyone what was going on. A coward, just like the night she'd first heard the howls.

It shouldn't have been Twig who got to be there when

this unicorn was born. It should've been Taylor or Janessa who witnessed such a wonder. Or even Mandy.

She put a hand on Wild Light's muscular back. She was so beautiful—perfectly if unusually formed, her coat moonlight white perfection. The old Twig never would have thought such wonders were possible. The old Twig had never had friends like the Murleys and their girls—or like Ben.

But what if she wasn't a new Twig at all? What if she was just pretending she was more? That she ever *could* be more?

She felt her tears, hot streaks on hotter cheeks. Not as hot as the burning lump in her heart. Feeling that lump again, she realized how long she'd been free of it. Even with all there was to fear on Lonehorn Island, she hadn't been weighed down by that searing, heavy lump of worthlessness. It had died down to an ember of pain she could barely sense, a mere ash waiting to be blown away by a new wind. But now it was back, in full flame.

She snapped the stall door shut without a word of explanation to Wild Light, without another glance. She ran outside, pulling on her hood and thinking only of sneaking back into the house and drawing her grass-green covers over her head. But Ben blocked her path.

"What happened?"

Twig shook her head.

"Twig! I didn't even hear her make a fuss."

"I can't do it."

"You didn't try. You gave up. You just gave up."

You said you wouldn't. He didn't say it. Didn't throw her words back at her, but he didn't have to.

She couldn't let him count on her. She would fail. Everything would go wrong, just like it always had for Twig Tupper.

"I thought I was someone new, but I'm not. I'm still Twig. Still the same."

"No," he said gruffly, "you're not somebody else."

Twig choked back a sob. She knew it. She knew it was true, but hearing Ben say it—

He grabbed one of her shoulders in each of his hands. "You're still Twig. But you're the Twig you were supposed to be. The Twig she needs you to be." He nodded back at the stable. "The Twig"—he let go of one of her shoulders and pushed her hood back and looked her in the eye—"I need you to be."

He turned away, and Twig knew there were tears in his eyes. Her own desire to cry evaporated. He was just as much afraid to fail as she was. Maybe this wasn't a worthless Twig thing, this fear. Maybe it didn't mean that she was still worthless Twig at all. She reached for his hand.

"I'll do it. I'll do it. Everything will be okay."

Ben's hand tightened around hers. "Come out riding. I want to see you come out riding."

"I will."

Twig walked briskly back to the stall and lifted the saddle out of the cedar shavings, then set it down again. She was supposed to be taming a unicorn. Wild Light had better have her horn. She ran one palm up Wild Light's forehead, found the smooth, round spot under her forelock with the other, and drew her horn out. Wild Light held her head even higher, and a new pride swirled in her quicksilver eyes.

"Wild Light," Twig said, loud and clear. Then she realized that she had no idea what to say next. She said a silent prayer that she wouldn't run out of the stall again, and she blurted the only thing she could think of. "You're a wonder. I'll be your rider and we'll ride into the darkness together and you'll be a wonder and a light. How would you like a new name? Wonder Light."

Wonder Light raised her forelegs and gave an eager neigh.

"Steady, girl. I'll call you Wonder for short, okay?"

She settled down, and with a deep breath, Twig picked up the saddle pad and laid it on her back. It would be a miracle if this worked.

When Twig added the saddle, Wonder stiffened and gave her a curious glance but didn't protest. The bitless bridle went on without incident. At least, with Mr. Murley's encouragement, she'd already gotten Wonder used to that, as well as a halter. But leading an animal around while walking was hardly the same as riding.

"You're such a good girl. Be my Wonder, please, girl." Twig gave her a big hug around her muscular neck, and then she led her out of the stall, into the stable aisle. "This is so important. I'm going to get on now. You'll let me ride, won't you?"

Would she? She was so headstrong. But Wonder nickered

and tickled Twig's neck. Twig slid a boot into the stirrup and hoisted herself up. Wonder whinnied questioningly, but she didn't resist. Twig buried her face in her mane and thanked her and told her what a good girl she was. Then she lifted her head and she gripped the reins and gave Wonder's sides a gentle squeeze.

Ben always said unicorns were smarter even than the smartest horse, and Twig had never doubted it was true. Wonder took a step forward. Twig urged her gently onward, through the stable and to the open door. She seemed to know exactly what Twig wanted, and she seemed to want it too.

Ben appeared in the doorway with a big grin on his face and pride gleaming in his eyes.

"I renamed her," Twig said shakily. "Wonder Light. From now on I'm going to call her Wonder."

"Perfect," Ben said. "She is a wonder." His voice caught. He cleared his throat and glanced at the ranch grounds behind him. "It's safe. I haven't heard or seen a thing. I'll go get the gate. Remember which way to go?"

"I remember."

She was supposed to take the long way around, behind

the buildings, through the far pastures, then follow the fence line to the gate and ride to the hollow. Merrill had taken Marble for a ride, away from the hollow, so Wonder wouldn't have to adjust to too many new things at once.

"Be good and quiet now, Wonder." Ben slipped her an acorn. "If she makes a fuss, dismount and try to lead her instead."

"She won't fuss."

"No." Ben stroked Wonder's flank. "I don't think she will."

Twig waited just outside the hollow until she saw Ben breathlessly approaching behind her. From the hollow, Indy neighed a curious, longing greeting, but stayed put, as he'd been taught. Twig was glad—Ben should be there when Indy met Wonder for the first time. Wonder sniffed and replied, anxiously leaping against Twig's attempts to hold her back.

Ben hurried to Indy, and Twig rode Wonder in. She dismounted, keeping hold of the young unicorn. But there was no need for concern. Wonder bowed her head, and Indy nuzzled his daughter, welcoming her to his side.

CHAPTER 31

ONCE THEY WERE OUTSIDE the fence and in the woods, Twig mounted Wonder again. Twig felt her own excitement echoed in Wonder's prance. The unicorn seemed to welcome the challenge, the chance to be like Indy. Wonder's muscles moved beneath Twig, ripples of energy that stirred her heart. She bounced straight up in the air, so high that Twig thought her insides would be left behind. Wonder landed and danced triumphantly.

I did it! I can jump like no one else, even with this girl on my back. No doubt Wonder would love to show this trick off to the ponies.

Indy, bearing Ben, neighed a calming warning, then bounded deeper into the woods. Wonder followed, more purposefully now, leaping just high enough to clear the underbrush, up and over, in a steady rhythm, copying Indy's pace. They glided through the mist, leaving Twig's troubles on the ground. Wonder was a streak of white, Twig's jacket no longer a shell but a wave of bright red, her hair flowing like Wonder's mane and tail.

But as they rode, the night grew mistier around them, the trees and the brambles harder to see. Wonder kept up her swift pace, her enthusiasm undaunted by the near-blinding mist. Twig's heart raced. The reins grew slick with the moisture in the air, her hands slippery with the cold sweat of fear.

The fog wrapped itself around them, cutting them off from Ben and Indy. They had to turn back, but she couldn't see. They were lost, caught in the web of mist, helpless prey.

Wonder tossed her head wildly.

"Ben!" Twig screamed.

Wonder leaped and reared. Twig lurched and lost the reins; she grasped at the chill winter air. She flew upward, grazing a tree branch, and then she was tumbling down. Leaves brushed her face and things crunched around her. Her elbow struck something hard. For a moment, she couldn't breathe. She waited for a howl, for a horn to strike.

A scuffle of hooves in the mist. Ben's muffled voice.

Hoof steps approached, but instead of a howl, there was a familiar nicker. Wonder nuzzled Twig's face, whinnying her concern. Ben, still riding Indy, held Wonder's reins.

"Twig? What happened?"

"That you, Ben-boy? What's going on?" Merrill's voice called in the distance. Marble whinnied anxiously.

"I'm all right." Twig wobbled to her feet, still shaking.

Light bobbed in the mist, and Merrill rode into view, Marble's reins in one hand, a lantern in the other.

Indy gave Marble a warning neigh. *This is my kid. Don't mess with her.*

Marble took a step back.

"So, Twig-girl," Merrill said, holding Marble steady, "how's that first ride going?"

Twig looked down at her boots.

"I took enough tumbles myself when I first started. It's a wonder you made it this far with a feisty young one like this. Never even known a saddle, has she?"

"That's what Twig's named her now—Wonder."

"Is that right? Don't you worry, Twig. You're the one who's given her what she needs since the day she was born. She's happy to give you her heart in return. But you must teach her how to know what you want, what you need."

"How to not toss me into the bushes." Twig rubbed her sore elbow.

Merrill laughed softly. "Yes. But you must learn to trust her at the same time. You were frightened by the mist?"

"I couldn't see Indy. I couldn't see anything."

"But Wonder could," Ben said.

"You're her rider. She felt your fear even more powerfully than Indy's lead."

"So she got spooked," Twig said.

"That's right." Marble whinnied at Wonder, and Merrill stroked his neck, calming him. "Why don't we let these two meet each other properly and then give it another try? You'll follow Ben and Indy. Just make a nice, wide circle, Ben, and come right back to me."

Twig hesitated.

Ben leaned down. "You can do this, Twig. You're her rider. It isn't easy in the mist, at night, over rough ground, but it's better this way, don't you think?"

"It's how I'll have to ride, if—when we go after Dagger."

"That's right," Merrill said. "You'll learn to ride, to stay on even when your unicorn charges."

"Eventually, you'll learn to shoot while you ride, like me."

It was so much, and there was so little time. Twig hopped back up into the saddle. She rubbed Wonder's neck. "We can do it," she whispered. "You're my Wonder after all."

• • •

Twig touched a fingertip gently to the fresh paint. It was dry enough. She couldn't stop thinking about last night, about leaning into Wonder's neck as she flew through the woods, about the way Wonder had begun to respond to her commands and her subtle nudges as she rode. She cleaned up her mess in the carport and picked up the wooden plaque. Balancing its edges between her fingertips, she carried it to the stable.

She paused at her pony's stall. "Hey there, Rain Cloud." He'd never been jealous of Wonder before. Would he now? The Murleys might not know what she and Ben were up to at night, but there was no hiding it from the ponies. Rain

Cloud had seemed to catch Indy's scent on Wonder when Twig brought her back to the stable. The unicorn and the pony had a little conversation about it. Twig was pretty sure that Rain Cloud knew the baby he'd watched over since her arrival had met her father.

Rain Cloud gave Twig an indignant blow.

"Come on, don't pout. I can't scratch your belly with my hands full. I'll be back."

Twig proceeded to the bigger stall at the end of the stable. Mr. Murley had taken Caper's plaque down recently and hung it in the den. Twig held the plaque she'd just painted up to the stall door, trying to eye the right spot, to make sure it looked just right. Wonder Light poked her head out and nuzzled Twig's neck. Twig laughed. The unicorn knew how to tickle her, and she returned Twig's laugh, as always, with her own nickery one.

Mr. Murley emerged from the tack room, whistling. "What've you got there, Twig?"

Twig held the plaque up. Her smile wavered and her hands shook a little. Mr. Murley came closer.

"Wonder Light?"

"That's her name."

"Not Wild Light?" he said gently, reaching out to tip up her chin with his hand.

"Not anymore. I like to call her Wonder."

Twig held her head up straight, the way the Murleys always wanted her to. She made herself look Mr. Murley right in the face, the way Ben did when he was being brave. "Will you help me put it on? We're sure about each other now. I know I can't start riding her right now, since she's so young..." Twig swallowed back the truth. The Murleys wouldn't understand that this creature wasn't like a horse of the same age, that she could be ridden. "But...since I'm going to be here for a while..."

They both knew she was asking for more than his help; she was asking for the beautiful little filly—now nearly a mare herself—that had taken the place of his beloved mare.

Mr. Murley put his arm around her shoulders. "Sure, Twig. I'll go and get my drill."

March

CHAPTER 32

I T WAS STILL MOSTLY dark when Twig stirred. She shut her eyes and tried to get back to sleep. How long had it been since she'd slipped back into bed? Sneaking out in the middle of the night to train Wonder with Ben and Merrill was really wearing on her. So was keeping it a secret. Mrs. Murley joked about her afternoon naps, teased that she was trying to get a jump-start on being a teenager. She wouldn't be able to joke about that for long; her thirteenth birthday was the day after tomorrow, the twenty-ninth of March.

She'd been out even longer than usual with Ben and Merrill, finalizing their plan of attack. Ben had been scouting on foot and found the area where the herd was resting during the day. Twig was supposed to sneak Wonder out of the pasture in the daytime, so they could catch Dagger by surprise, hopefully still in a sleepy winter state. She just had to come up with something to tell the Murleys so they wouldn't come looking for her...

There was a loud sniffle, and Twig realized a warm little lump was curled up next to her in her bed.

"Casey?" Twig wriggled her arm around her and pulled her closer. "Bad dream?"

Casey shook her head. "I couldn't sleep. The howls..."

Twig shot up. "They were close?"

"Uh-huh."

"How close?"

Casey shuddered. "Close as they could get."

Twig jumped out of bed and yanked the curtains aside, peering into the predawn darkness. The stable doors were shut. Everything looked normal. Had the herd attacked? Had Ben and Merrill stopped them? She had to make sure they were okay. Twig rushed outside without her shell, running through a fine, misty rain. It was so warm, almost as warm as yesterday. This year, spring had come early to Lonehorn Island.

She climbed over the fence, but it was slippery and she lost her balance. Something sharp jabbed into her hand.

Twig dropped to the ground and examined her palm. An ugly splinter had pierced the skin, sending a trickle of blood down her wrist. A wedge was ripped out of the fence rail. The ground was trampled.

With a gasp, Twig pulled the splinter out, then slipped into the woods, headed for Ben's hollow.

"Ben?" Her voice was high with fear for him.

"I'm all right, Twig."

Twig ducked into the hollow. Ben was alone, rubbing Indy down. The unicorn was shaking.

"What about Merrill?"

"He's fine. But Marble isn't."

Marble! Marble, who'd come so far, bonding with Merrill, letting him ride. "Is he—"

"He's alive, but barely."

"Where?"

"Merrill took him through the passage. He's going to find somewhere to hide him there until he's better."

If he gets better. If he isn't discovered. Taken, for the queen's army. Merrill, sent to the Barrenlands.

"He'd die for sure here," Ben said. "He cannot defend himself."

"What about the ranch? You left Wonder there for

safekeeping. Couldn't we take Marble there? I could say I found him."

"One unicorn on the ranch is risky. Two is impossible. Their horns would extend, and they'd be given away."

Of course. "If Wind Catcher hadn't…"

"I'd planned on taking Wind Catcher back out as soon as I could. I was desperate to keep her safe while I took care of my father, especially in her condition. And then, it seemed the perfect solution for her filly. She'd be fed and cared for, safe inside the stable at night."

Ben looked away, but not before she saw the fear in his eyes, that Wonder was no longer safe inside that stable at night.

"They tried to break through the fence."

"I know." Twig reached for his arm. "It wasn't a mistake, Ben. Wonder and me…"

He nodded.

But what were they going to do now? They were down one unicorn and rider, just when Twig and Wonder were ready to do their part—just when they'd planned to take out Dagger.

"We can still do it, Ben."

Ben shook his head. "I promised Merrill I'd wait for him."

"It'll be too late!"

"It's too late already! They're up. They're hunting."

Twig glared at him, then rubbed roughly at the tears that escaped down her cheeks.

Ben straightened up and tried to sound brave. "We'll just have to come up with a new plan, that's all. We'll figure it out, Twig."

• • •

Twig leaned back on the couch with her book, trying to concentrate. She'd chosen it from the list of classics Mrs. Murley had given her. She was supposed to have a book report written on it by the end of next week.

"I hate that book." Mandy, sitting on the floor nearby, made a face.

Twig glowered at her. She'd thought she would hate it too, but the story had soon swept her away. It had been hard to put down until now. Now she couldn't stop thinking about Ben and Indy.

"He dies, you know."

Twig jolted. Regina stood over her. She nodded at Twig's book.

"He does not!" Next to Twig, Casey thunked her own book onto the side table in protest.

"How do you know? You haven't read it," Regina said. "You're still reading baby books!"

Casey's lip quivered.

Mandy frowned sympathetically.

"It's all right, Casey, you're getting better every day. Isn't she, Janessa?" Taylor reached up from the rug to pat Casey's knee.

"They're not baby books! I like that series." Janessa popped up from her own pillow on the floor. "Time travel! Magic…"

But Twig threw her book at Regina, grabbed Casey's hand, and stormed out of the house. She stood there on the porch, clutching Casey's hand, chest heaving. *He doesn't die*, she kept telling herself. *He doesn't.*

"Who cares?" Twig said. "Who cares about any of them?"

Casey stared up at her with those big, tear-filled eyes. She cared. They both cared. And caring hurt. Caring was as dangerous as the creatures lurking in the shadows of the cedars.

•••

Twig lay in bed, waiting for the Murleys to go to sleep so she could sneak out and join Ben in protecting the ranch. Ben had come to the paddock fence and told her that Merrill had sent word. He'd found a hiding place for Marble and he'd be back tomorrow. They just had to get through tonight without him.

Twig listened for signs of wakefulness in the house. And then she heard it—a faint banging. The sound grew louder, more persistent—too deep and too distant to be someone knocking on the door. *Bang, bang, bang*—then a sharp *crack* and a tremendous *crash*!

Twig jumped up, and Casey woke with a wail. The sounds had come from outside, and now a series of cries, muffled by the stable walls, took their place—fearful pony wails and a louder, fiercer whinny. Wonder Light! Twig bolted to the window and tore at the curtains. A group of large animal forms leap-galloped through the mist. The wild herd.

"They're here!" Twig gasped. "They got in!"

CHAPTER 33

THROUGH THE BLUR OF fog, Twig thought she saw one of the unicorns dip its head and charge at the stable door.

Bang! Bang! They were going to break into the stable next.

Twig ran from the room with a groggy, weepy Casey stumbling after her. Mrs. Murley was already in the entryway with her boots on. Mr. Murley was barefoot, but his shotgun was in his hands. He threw the door open, and it bashed against the wall. The other girls, who'd all come tumbling out of bed after them, jumped.

"Stay here, girls!" Mrs. Murley shut the door firmly behind Mr. Murley.

Twig grabbed her boots.

A gunshot cracked the air. The entryway walls shook with the boom, and the sound reverberated in Twig's chest. She dropped her boot. Janessa froze with her jacket half on.

Mr. Murley fired again. Twig recovered, ducked past Mrs. Murley, and reached for the door, but just as she did, it flew open.

Mr. Murley's face was ash white.

"David! What is it?"

"Something's smashed right through the fence!"

"What?"

"Wild horses," Mr. Murley said, but he didn't sound convinced. "It was hard to see in the fog. They were circling the stable. Circling it like prey. Howling like hounds. When I fired, they ran off. They're gone for now. They're gone."

"I told you I heard things howling!" Mandy said. "I told you!"

Twig shoved her foot into her boot, scrunching her sock awkwardly under her heel. She bolted out the door, her shell dangling from her arm, one sleeve on, one off.

She was halfway to the stable when a lone, high whinny-howl cut through the mist. The Murleys and their girls, all running across the lawn behind her, stopped shouting

Twig's name and gasped. Then, an eerie chorus joined the howl, and the ever-unconcerned Regina burst loudly into tears.

"What is it? What's that noise?" Mandy cried. "Horses don't make that noise!"

Janessa clamped her hands over her ears, and Taylor, who always looked stern, tried to look stern *and* brave. She scooched closer to Regina and put an arm around her. Casey didn't say a word; she just sprinted to Twig's side and slipped her hand into Twig's.

Twig's heart was pounding, pounding. Should she get Ben? What if he was already here? What if Mr. Murley misunderstood and shot him?

Twig tried to let go of Casey's hand and hurry the rest of the way to the stable, but Casey hung on tight, so Twig dragged her along. The stable door was scarred and scratched, raw wood showing pale and woundlike through the deep red paint. Here and there were dents made with the point of a hard, sharp instrument—a horn. Twig put her finger in one. It wasn't just a dent; it was a hole. Her finger went all the way through. She unlatched the door, ran in, and flipped the main light switch, flooding the stable with light.

Mrs. Murley and the other girls followed her inside while Mr. Murley stood at the door with his shotgun ready, alternately squinting at the damage and at the mist-shrouded woods surrounding the property.

The ponies were quaking and crying out pitifully with fear, but still safe in their stalls. But Wonder wasn't quaking; she was rearing and kicking at her stall door in an absolute fury.

Mrs. Murley shouted a warning to Twig, but Twig said, "Casey, get me some tack. Hurry!"

Twig dug through the pile of cedar shavings in the corner of Wonder's stall and pulled out the sword she'd begun hiding there once it got close to springtime.

By the time Casey emerged, staggering, with an armful of tack, Twig was wearing her scabbard and she had Wonder in the aisle, her frenzy restrained to an anxious pacing.

"My bow and quiver!" Twig said. "Quick!"

Casey ran back to the tack room, where Twig kept the bow.

Twig got Wonder saddled up while Mrs. Murley tried to talk some sense into her. But Mrs. Murley was too wary of Wonder in her agitated state to get close. Each time Mrs. Murley attempted to touch Twig, Wonder snapped a toothy warning. Breathless, Casey handed Twig the bow and quiver.

"You need to stay here, Twig," Mrs. Murley said. "Just let Mr. Murley handle it."

"He can't. Not this."

"Twig, do you know something about this?"

Twig paused with her foot in the stirrup. "Maybe."

"What is *that*?" Mrs. Murley pointed to the scabbard.

Twig didn't answer. Mrs. Murley's hands dropped to her sides. She stared at Twig and Wonder. Twig mounted and rode out of the stable. "Just keep the ponies in and fix the fence," she called as she passed Mr. Murley. "Don't come after me. Don't go out there! I'll be back!"

Mrs. Murley came to her senses. She darted out after her, shouting, "Twig!"

"You let her go?" Mr. Murley said helplessly. "Why did you let her go?"

"I don't know! Oh God! I don't know. David, *what* is going on?"

Twig just rode on, fighting back her tears. She wanted to yell for Ben, but his secret was still a secret and not hers to tell. Just before she reached the broken section of fence, Twig glanced back and saw Mr. Murley hand his shotgun to Mrs. Murley and run into the stable. He was going to get Feather, going to come after her.

She rode Wonder through the jagged gap where the herd had broken through the fence and into the thick, terrifying blackness of the forest.

"Ben!" she screamed. "Ben! Are you there?"

Twig held Wonder steady and listened. She could still hear the howls, but they were growing increasingly distant, and they had a different, more frightened sound. Those gunshots had really scared them off. Maybe they were safer than she'd feared, at least for now—as long as Mr. Murley stayed on watch with his shotgun. Maybe she should go back before he left the ranch and tell him so.

A blur of movement caught her eye. A unicorn. Wonder's forelock parted as her sharp white horn extended in response to its presence. Twig stiffened and had a fleeting argument with herself whether to run or to hide. But Wonder gave the creature a whinny—strained, but a greeting just the same.

Indy flowed around the underbrush like a silver-white

stream, then drew alongside her. Ben's face was hard and determined, his cheeks flushed, his cloak pushed back, and his hair dripping with sweat.

"They broke through the fence and then they tried to break down the stable door."

Ben nodded. "I heard gunshots."

"That was Mr. Murley. I don't think he got any of them, but he scared them off."

"They'll keep their distance, but I don't know how long. Not when they're like this."

"Mr. Murley's coming. He doesn't understand what's going on. He's trying to protect me."

"He needs to stay there, to shoot if they come back. He needs to stay there!"

"I know. I have to go back, then. He won't leave me out here."

"And I have to get to the passage. We're not safe here anymore, me and Indy. And neither is she." Ben nodded at Wonder.

Dread hung as heavy in Twig's heart as the mist around the passage to Terracornus.

"But they're not safe in Terracornus either. You said—"

"I can take them to Merrill. He'll hide them for a while, while I figure things out. Here, right now, they'll die. Dagger is out for blood—their blood. Could be they'll attack those ponies, just because Dagger's got them hungry for a kill. But Wonder's the one who's been driving Dagger to a frenzy. The last couple days have brought out the spring in her, something new in her scent. She's the offspring of his rival. Even for a normal unicorn, it's his instinct to kill her. And Dagger—"

"You have to take her with you. You have to!" Twig gripped Wonder's mane in her hands along with the reins. "And you can't take them both by yourself. I have to come."

Ben nodded slowly, solemnly. "Yes, if you want to save her, you'll have to come."

"I'll come. I'll be right back."

"Twig!" Ben protested.

But she wheeled Wonder around and urged her back toward the ranch. Wonder flew through the forest at her strange, fluid, leaplike gallop, a creature made to flow in and out of the cedars like the island's breath.

Just before they reached the fence line, Twig pulled Wonder back abruptly and pressed her horn back down.

"Mr. Murley!" she called into the fog. "I'm here! I'm here! Come back!"

Mrs. Murley came running toward her, a shadow in the mist, surrounded by a circle of flashlight glow. Her form sharpened as she and Twig closed the space between them. She didn't have the shotgun.

"Twig!" Mrs. Murley said with relief. Then she pulled her phone out and desperately dialed Mr. Murley's cell while all the girls ran to the fence, flashlights bobbing in their hands, yelling for him.

Twig rode into the yard. "Get in the house! Everyone get in the house and lock the doors!" But the girls ran toward her and Wonder instead.

Mrs. Murley held her phone to her tear-streaked face. "David?"

Oh, thank God. He'd answered.

"Yes. She's here. Come back. Hurry."

Seconds later, he galloped up the driveway. Janessa and Taylor threw the gate open for him, then shut it behind him. The shotgun was balanced across his lap, held steady with one hand, Feather's reins in the other.

"You have to stay here," Twig said. "Please. And I have to go."

"Go?"

"I'll come back. There's something I have to take care

of. But I'll come back." Her voice broke on the last word because she knew that she might not—not if the island's herd had its way.

Mr. Murley pulled Feather right in front of Wonder. He shone his own flashlight, the small one he kept in his pocket, on Twig. "I won't let you go, Twig. I don't know what's going on here, but there's no way you're going back into those woods. Now get down and put that horse back in the stable, and we'll figure this out."

Twig opened her mouth to protest, but behind her, Regina screamed. Mandy gasped, and Wonder whirled around. A figure was running across the yard, headed right for them.

"It's him!" Casey said, a hint of triumph mixed with the awe and the surprise. "The wild boy!"

Ben's cloak billowed out behind him as he flew toward them, on foot. His quiver bounced on his back and his scabbard swung at one side, his pouch at the other.

Mr. Murley jolted, and Twig cried, "Ben! He's my friend, Mr. Murley."

"Your friend?"

Ben stopped a few yards away. He regarded Mr.

Murley with a look half wary, half bold. He was out in the open—there were no shadows, no trees, no eaves, and no cover of night, for half a dozen flashlight beams shone right at him through the mist—but he stood there in the yard and he lifted his chin and he held his shoulders back.

Casey smiled, and Mrs. Murley grabbed her hand, as though she were afraid she'd take off too, and pulled her close to her side.

"It's all right, Twig," Ben said. "Show them."

"Show them?"

He gave her a nod. She slid her hand under Wonder's mane and drew her horn out. The girls screamed and grabbed at each other.

Mr. Murley almost fell off Feather. He stumbled over to Twig and Wonder.

"Crazy Uncle Matt," he said breathily. "You weren't crazy after all. 'You've got to keep that island.' That's what he kept saying before he died. He made me promise I wouldn't sell it. 'For the other Murleys,' he said, 'in case they want to come back.'"

"Back?" Twig said.

"From the land of unicorns," Mrs. Murley said in a lost sort of whisper. "That's where you went, isn't it, Twig?"

"That's where I'm going."

"I'll bring her back," Ben said.

"I wouldn't go if it wasn't important," Twig added.

No one said anything. No one moved. Then Ben cupped his hands and called out to the woods. A neigh answered, and in a moment Indy came galloping through the mist. He slowed to a trot at the edge of the crowd. His great horn was extended, and the water droplets left on it by the misty air reflected back the flashlight beams like something shimmering and magic.

Ben mounted with a perfect swiftness that seemed nearly as magical.

"I love you," Twig called over her shoulder as she followed Ben and Indy. "I love all of you."

The woods were so black, squeezing around them, but Indy knew the way, and Wonder knew just how to follow her father. Twig held on tight and tried to trust her unicorn, even as the howling grew louder.

The brush rustled. Wonder cried out, and Indy answered with a warning neigh. Just ahead, the branches parted, and Twig saw the horn, dark as midnight. The edge of its spiraling rib glistened razor sharp with the wet of the gloom. Dagger!

CHAPTER 34

WONDER PIVOTED AND DARTED to the side. To Twig's horror, Dagger dipped his head to attack. She couldn't see the menacing horn; she could only imagine it piercing Wonder's side, slashing at her own legs. Dagger was going to charge.

Dagger let out an outraged utterance of pain, and Twig glanced back. Indy was there, raising his horn, stained dark and wet. Ben shouted commandingly at Indy and gave him his heels, urging him out of Dagger's reach, though it was clear that his unicorn's desire was to stay and fight.

Dagger lurched after Indy. The gash on his flank forced him to take a slower, more awkward stride, but it wasn't enough to stop him. Wonder sidestepped, wavering between her fear—her urge to flee and survive—and her desire to defend her father. Then she sprinted to Indy's side.

Dagger paused and howled into the night. Several howls answered him, so close. In the distance, more responded. The herd was coming.

Twig struggled to nock an arrow and take aim. Dagger turned, his lip curled back. It looked like he was smiling in anticipation as he leaped, nimbly as ever, toward the sound of his approaching herd.

Twig's arrow whooshed toward Dagger, then arched down, just behind Dagger's flank. It cut through the ferns and stuck in the ground.

"Hurry! To the passage!" Ben cried.

As they wove through the trees and the brush, some of the shadows in the thickening mist began to move with them. Wonder's eyes widened, but she seemed too afraid to even make the usual sounds of fear. Wonder's and Indy's ears flattened back completely. They galloped side by side, communicating silently to each other.

The shadows took form. They called out high cries of hunger, and they broke through the brush, headed straight for Wonder and Indy.

In a blink, Dagger was at Wonder's flanks, and this time, Indy wasn't in position to rescue her. Wonder, the born jumper, leaped like never before. Twig's fear-tightened stomach flopped as she hung on. When Wonder landed, her hooves met firmer ground. They'd reached the clearing in the mist around the hemlock circle. Ben pulled Indy back to let Twig go ahead.

But Wonder reared at the seemingly impassable branches, no matter how Twig urged her to go—until Ben rode Indy right through. Then Wonder followed, crying out her protest.

Ben dismounted. "I have to open the door. Get down. You'll have to lead her through the passage."

Ben took out the key. Twig dismounted and snatched up Wonder's lead.

On the other side of the hemlocks, the wild unicorns stopped and screamed at the bristling branches.

"They don't want to come through. They don't want to go to Terracornus," Ben said breathlessly.

They didn't want to push their way through the boughs, to feel the needles scratching at their noses and their eyes, or, to hear Ben tell it, enter some distant nightmare beyond the passage, but their desire to kill Indy and Wonder was strong.

"Hurry, Ben! Hurry anyway!"

The key clicked in the lock, and Ben threw the door open and gave Indy a slap on the hindquarters that sent him reluctantly but obediently through. Then Ben joined Twig in trying to talk Wonder into following. Wonder tossed her head in confusion and protest.

"She's never been there," Twig said. "Why won't she go?"

"She was made for this world, not that one, and she knows it." Ben gave Wonder a harsh slap on the rump, and she bolted forward so fast that Twig barely had time to dive out of the way.

Twig ran after Wonder and snatched her reins just as she emerged in the mist on the other side. Ben slammed and locked the door behind them. Twig leaned back against the tree trunk, digging her fingers into the rough bark. Her heart was beating so fast, her breath quick and gaspy.

Ben emerged from the tunnel inside the cedar and slipped the key back under his shirt. Twig stumbled back to examine the tree. It was hard to see in the fog, but it looked like it was the exact same tree on Lonehorn Island, only on this side, the Terracornus side, the arched opening in the tree had no door.

Twig was standing on a narrow dirt road that led to that opening. A pink and orange glow filtered through the mist surrounding the tree. "What is that light?"

Ben glanced around him, confused, then said, "Oh. It's the sunset."

"Sunset?" Twig gasped.

"It's a different world, a different time. Breathe deep, Twig. Make yourself breathe deep."

Twig nodded. She tried. The air was so heavy with moisture. Her legs were rubber. No, they were wet paper. They dissolved under her. She'd never ridden so hard in her life. But then she'd just ridden *for* her life. And she'd ridden into another world.

Ben fished a flask of water out of his pouch. He squatted in front of her. She tried to take the flask and drink when he offered it, but her hand shook and sloshed it.

"Not just yet, I think." Ben screwed the cap back on but left it in her hands. "You hold on to it and give yourself a minute."

"I'm sorry, girl," Ben told Wonder. "We'll get you back there soon.

"They all know it somewhere inside," he said to Twig,

"and every unicorn born in Terracornus spends his life longing to find this passage."

Twig listened to Ben talk soothingly to both of the unicorns. He told them about the nice fresh water he was going to lead them to once they'd caught their breath. Twig shut her eyes and breathed deeply the strange, musty air, and let him calm her too.

Twig opened her eyes again, and she drank a gulp of cold, metallic water. She stood up on weak but steadier legs and passed the flask to Ben.

He took a long drink, then stopped himself and screwed the lid back on. "We've got to get going now. There's a stream not far from here, where we can rest and water the unicorns."

The road took a sharp turn not far ahead, and she couldn't make out where it went, couldn't see anything but forest. Along the roadside, tall, upright trees with smooth, silvery bark were interspersed with broader, smaller trees with birchlike white trunks and branches swelling with pale green leaf buds.

Twig walked over to a wooden post a few yards ahead, where the road branched off. Two signs were nailed to it.

Beneath the engraved words "Dead-End Tree," an arrow on one of the signs pointed to the passage they'd just come through. The other sign pointed to the well-worn branch of road ahead and suggested, in cheerful green paint, the way to "Clover Gully."

The stretch of road between the passage tree and the signs was rocky and weedy, but the roads beyond the signs were well maintained, well traveled. By who? The queen's army? Unicorn killers?

Ben called to Emmie. A coo answered him from the branches of the passage tree, and she fluttered down. He scattered some seed on the ground for her, then took a scrap of paper and a stick that resembled thick pencil lead from his pouch and scrawled something. He rolled the paper tight and began to slip it into the tube on Emmie's leg. He stopped, frowned, and pulled something out of the tube.

"Is it a note from Merrill?" Twig said.

Ben's eyes flicked from the note to Twig. He turned his back and quickly read it, then stuffed it in his pouch.

"What is it?"

"Nothing."

But Twig knew it wasn't nothing.

"Go see Merrill now," he told Emmie. "Let him know we're on our way."

On their way to bring him two unicorns to hide from whatever was out there, in the inscrutable forest beyond the mist, full of secrets Ben was keeping from her. Twig shivered in her shell. All she wanted was to be in that warm yellow house. Safe in her bed. But no one was safe in bed at Island Ranch. Not with the herd awake and hungry.

"Wait!" Twig grabbed Ben's arm, just as Emmie took flight. "Call her back! Tell Merrill to come help us."

"But—"

Twig fumbled for Wonder's mist-wet reins. "I'm going back."

Ben's eyes widened. "You cannot," he protested. But he called Emmie.

"Dagger is out for blood. You said so yourself. What do you think he'll do when Indy and Wonder don't come back? Just give up?"

Ben looked at the ground, and Twig knew she was right.

"He'll go back to the ranch, looking for Wonder. Him and his herd. Her scent is there, isn't it? He already killed one horse. The girls won't just stay inside and let him do it again. They won't."

Emmie landed on Ben's shoulder. He lifted his head. He shifted his cloak. "They'll fight."

Twig nodded, a lump forming in her throat. Those girls were fighters, every one of them, and the Murleys too.

"What if Mr. Murley can't shoot them all? What if he *does* shoot them all? The herd will be gone."

Ben removed the message from Emmie's leg and dug the pencil out of his pouch. The crumpled note he'd just read wafted to the ground, but Ben didn't notice. As he scrawled on the paper again, revising his message to Merrill, Twig carefully stepped on the dropped note. Ben turned to send Emmie off, and Twig bent down, as though to adjust her boot. She picked up the note and slipped it into the pocket of her shell.

Ben watched Emmie disappear into the sunset beyond the mist.

"We can't wait for Merrill." Twig tried to sound resolved, but her voice shook.

Ben met her eyes, and she gave him her stubbornest glare.

"Here." Ben ducked his head through the leather cord around his neck and tossed the key to Twig.

It caught her by surprise, and she had to fumble in the dirt for it.

"You unlock the door, and I'll ride through first. I'll distract them while you and Wonder run for the ranch."

"Wait for me under the tree, Ben, please. At least until I've mounted again."

He shook his head. "I want to take them by surprise."

The walk back to the Dead-End Tree was over too quickly—or not quickly enough. As she fitted the key into the lock, Twig pressed her ear to the door. She could hear them—wild unicorns, calling, pawing, stamping, even sniffing.

"They're here. They're so close." What if, in their moments of waiting and pacing, they had dared to brave the branches? What if they were right outside the door now, under the tree? Twig listened again, but the door was thick, and it was impossible to tell.

"Hurry!" Ben said.

"Can they smell us on the other side? If they can, they won't be surprised."

"Twig!" he said insistently.

She turned the key and threw the door open, and Wonder raised a hoof, poised to bolt out.

"No!" Twig cried, and Ben grabbed Wonder's bridle and ordered her back, to the side.

As soon as Twig took Wonder's reins, Ben led Indy through the tunnellike hollow in the tree trunk and out the door, then mounted. Indy squealed his indignation as he and Ben broke through the sweeping branches of the hemlocks, but they barely slowed.

Twig hurried to mount Wonder, as screams pierced the fog and Ben and Indy clashed with whatever was waiting for them on the other side. But Wonder was in a near frenzy of pawing and screaming. Fearing for Ben, Twig mounted anyway. As soon as she did, as soon as she let Wonder leap through the mist, the unicorn's protest stopped. She was focused, determined, as she broke through the branches and into the fray.

CHAPTER 35

ONE UNICORN LAY ON the ground, an arrow pro-
truding from its flank. It jerked its head to avoid
the crushing blows of Indy's hooves. A long gash on
its foreleg gushed as Indy kicked, punishing it for every attempt to rise. Ben leaned back hard and steered
Indy away.

Another unicorn came leaping at them, and Twig let go
the reins, clinging to Wonder with her thighs as she fired
an arrow. This one struck its target, piercing the creature's
side. The unicorn screamed and stumbled away, into the
brush. Twig froze, feeling sick.

"Go, Twig! Hurry!"

"No! You'll never get away on your own. Besides," Twig
said with a new certainty, "Wonder wants to fight." It was
true. She could feel it.

Ben gave her a curt nod. "We stay together then, and head for the ranch."

Another unicorn darted into the circle of mist. Twig urged Wonder toward it, but when the wild unicorn saw Wonder, it retreated, giving a long, high, lingering neigh—a call into the distance. Far away, another unicorn answered.

"I know that call," Ben said. "It's Dagger! He's coming!"

Wonder neighed a desperate neigh—not desperately afraid, but desperately eager. Twig felt her unicorn's urge to fight rippling through every muscle beneath her. She sat up straighter, shouldered her bow, and gripped the reins with white knuckles.

"Then let's go to him!" Twig said. Enough running, enough waiting for the perfect moment. Enough of waking up, trembling in the dead of night. It was time to deal with Dagger.

Ignoring Ben's protest, she let Wonder run, this time not in flight, but in pursuit. It was her turn to hunt. Ben followed close behind, and Indy neighed his encouragement to his daughter. Wonder leaped, higher, longer than she ever had, higher even, than Indy. Twig's insides felt strange and light; she forgot the feel of the reins clutched tight in her hands; she forgot the ache of her legs straining to hold on, forgot the tenseness of fear. All she knew was that she was flying. Wonder's hooves finally met the earth some thirty feet from where they'd left it, and she sprang up into the air again in the same instant.

Twig caught a blur of movement—Dagger, his horn dark as midnight, poised to strike, leaping through the air right across her path. Wonder, in midleap, cried out. Behind Twig, Ben and Indy cried out too. Wonder swerved in the air, but so did Dagger. A throb of impact. Twig jolted. And then they were falling.

Dagger's horn had struck. Wonder crashed into the brush, and Twig hurtled over Wonder's head and managed to tuck her own head just in time. Twig's shoulder hit the ground hard, and her knee struck the root of a tree. Wonder sprang back to her feet. There was a long, shallow gash across her side, but no puncture. Wonder had collided with Dagger, but she'd managed to maneuver a would-be fatal blow into a glance.

"Twig!"

As soon as she turned toward the shout, Twig saw the

shadow arching over her. She flattened herself into the ferns as Dagger leaped over her. He landed just feet away. Wonder whirled on him and their horns clashed with a bone-jarring sound. Indy kicked at Dagger's flank with his rear legs and Ben threw his knife. It lodged in Dagger's side, and Dagger screamed and turned toward Ben and Indy. When he did, Wonder charged.

Wonder's horn drove into Dagger's shoulder, and Dagger swished his head to the side violently, slashing at Wonder. Twig desperately called her back. Whether simply to withdraw her horn and prepare for another strike or out of obedience, Wonder pulled back.

Twig leaped onto Wonder's back and circled her away from Dagger. Indy was getting some distance too. Twig locked eyes with Ben.

"Go ahead," he said. His bow was in his hand, and he was trying to hold Indy steady while readying an arrow.

Twig understood. Dagger was on his feet again, wavering but frothing with ferocity. She gave Wonder a running start and she charged at Dagger.

Twig leaned hard into Wonder's neck, putting everything she had into staying attached to her unicorn's back.

She felt the plunge but could see nothing with her face buried in the silver silk of Wonder's mane. She jerked to a stop. Dagger shrieked, and then Wonder withdrew again. With a whoosh, Ben's arrow flew, and it lodged in Dagger's side not far from the wound Wonder had just inflicted.

Twig circled away from the writhing wild unicorn. Ben dismounted and drew his sword and ordered Indy to stay back. Slowly, he advanced on Dagger. Twig dismounted too. Wonder had done her job well, done her share; her horn was stained with blood. And Twig wanted no more of that.

As she calmed Wonder, Twig peered into the midnight-black eyes of Dagger, and her heart skipped a beat. He let out a soft, pleading wail, and those eyes seemed to plead with her too.

"Ben," she said, "wait."

Ben flicked a sideways glance at her without moving his head or his sword. He turned his eyes, which had been filled with readiness and near rage, back to Dagger with a new kind of scrutiny—far from trusting, but ready to consider.

Ben took a deep breath, and he tipped the blade aside. "Well," he said quietly to Dagger, "are we done?"

The unicorn's eyes stayed wild and wide. Was it more with fear now, than with hunger for the kill? Ben took a step backward. Indy gave a snort of new fury. Ben turned to him and put a calming hand on his muzzle. When he did so, Dagger shot to his feet with an explosion of power. His horn was tipped and ready to drive right through Ben's back.

Twig shrieked, and as she did, she drew her sword and thrust up. She gripped the hilt with both hands. It struck resistance and she thrust harder. The unicorn screamed a terrifying call of pain and fear and threat. Twig yelped, letting go of her sword and falling out of reach of the flailing hooves. Ben jumped out of the way.

Indy charged at Dagger, but the stallion knew it was too late; Twig's sword had already done the job. Indy tilted his horn at Dagger, but he didn't stab.

Wonder was at Twig's side, pawing the ground near her, entreating her.

"I'm okay, girl." Twig rose on shaky legs. She gave Wonder a kiss. "I'm okay."

She hadn't meant to kill Dagger, hadn't had room for anything in her head or her heart other than *Don't kill Ben. Don't.*

Ben put a boot on Dagger's chest to brace himself as he withdrew Twig's sword. He wiped it on the branches and then handed it to her. "Thank you. You saved my life."

Twig took the sword. She let it hang limp at her side as she stared at Dagger. His body shuddered much as Wind Catcher's had. Then it stilled. "I don't know if I'm glad or not."

Ben put an arm around her shoulder. "*I'm* glad. I'm sorry you had to do it, but I'm glad he's gone."

"You gave him another chance."

"I thought I saw a little bit of Midnight Dream. But what he did, in the end…he's the one who let the Dagger in him win."

Howls faded into the distance. The rest of the herd was in retreat. Had Dagger insisted on coming after his enemies alone this time, or faced with opposing unicorns and their determined riders, had the herd chosen not to follow him?

"What about the rest of them?"

"There's still a lot of work to do. This herd will be looking for a new leader. If the wrong one takes the role, this will be all for nothing."

The sound of movement through the brush sent Twig

and Ben scrambling for their weapons. But Merrill's voice called out, "Ben?"

"Here, Merrill!"

Merrill appeared, bow in hand. "Two dead back at the passage," he announced. "One more badly wounded, but she managed to retreat with the others. Is that him? Dagger?"

"It's him," Ben replied.

Merrill took a step closer to inspect the creature who had turned so many midnights into nightmares for all of Lonehorn Island. "Well done," he said. "Well done."

CHAPTER 36

WHEN TWIG AND BEN rode up to the ranch, five girls came running for the driveway gate, crying, "Twig, Twig! She's back!"

Twig dismounted and enveloped Casey in a hug.

"You were gone so long," Casey said.

"Don't worry," Taylor said with an air of even more responsibility than usual, "no one called the police."

Regina said, "They talked about it a lot, though."

Casey let Twig go, and she wiped a hand across her dark eyes.

"I'm back now. Everything's going to be okay now."

Twig led Wonder through the gate. Mr. and Mrs. Murley were hurrying, side by side, down the driveway, toward her. Twig turned to say good-bye to Ben before he rode away, but to her surprise, he had dismounted too. He shifted his feet.

Twig gestured with her head for Ben to come. She shouldn't have even considered letting him return to the wilds of the island by himself. Now that everyone at Island Ranch knew about the unicorns, there was no sense in him being all alone.

First Mrs. Murley, then Mr. Murley gave Twig a long, hard hug. The girls stood around in awed silence, trying not to make it too obvious that they were staring at Ben.

When the Murleys released her, Twig said, "Dagger, the leader of the wild herd—he's dead."

"You should be proud of Twig," Ben put in. "She killed him, and she saved my life doing it."

The girls gasped. Mrs. Murley's mouth fell open.

Mr. Murley said, "Twig?" and Twig blushed and couldn't decide whether she was furious with Ben for blabbing about it or whether she wanted to hug him.

"Everyone here owes their lives to *you*," Twig said, with a great effort not to stammer. "You and your father kept everyone safe—safe from things no one else wanted to think about."

Mr. Murley squinted at Ben. "What's your name, young man?"

"Ben."

Mr. Murley swallowed visibly. "Ben what?"

Twig was about to say, "Just Ben," but Ben stood up straighter and looked Mr. Murley right in the eye. "Ben Murley, sir. My father's name was Darian—a name from Terracornus—you've probably never heard of him. But his grandfather's name was Elijah Murley."

"Elijah Murley!" Mrs. Murley said. "One of Edward Murley's lost sons."

"Of course," Mr. Murley said. "Of course. Your father— you said, 'was'?"

"He died," Ben said quickly. "Last year."

Mrs. Murley murmured, "Oh, Ben."

"You're a Murley. You're welcome here. Why don't we put your...unicorns"—Mr. Murley smiled in sheepish astonishment as he said the word—"in the stable and get them cleaned up and taken care of, and then you can come inside with us for a while."

Ben was a Murley? What other secrets was he keeping? The note! She felt in her pocket. It was still there. With everyone's attention on Ben, she sneaked it out. Cupping it in her hand, she made out a few cryptic lines in Merrill's handwriting.

It's worse than I feared here. As soon as we've dealt with Dagger, you must come to Westland. For the sake of all unicorns, all Terracornus, you must appeal to the queen.

What did it mean? Clearly there was more to it than concern over Marble's safety. Was Ben going to leave soon? What was going on in Terracornus? The last thing Twig wanted to do right now was leave the ranch. But if it meant helping the unicorns, she had to go with him into that strange land beyond the passage. She had to do everything she could to help him before she had to leave the island for good.

"Twig?" Casey said.

"I'm coming."

Twig tucked the note back in her pocket. She'd talk to Ben about it later. For now, she just wanted to be home, to be happy.

•••

Twig ate the last bite of her sandwich and took a drink of orange juice. The rest of the girls had already eaten. They were all outside with Ben, except for Casey. She wouldn't leave Twig's side. Casey had been there, in their room, waiting even though the afternoon sun was glaring through the curtains by the time Twig woke up. Last night, Twig had taken care of Wonder, then collapsed into bed.

Mrs. Murley picked up Twig's plate. "Why don't I take that for you, Twig, and you can call your stepmother?"

Twig put down her glass. "Call Keely?"

"She called while you were sleeping, to wish you a happy birthday."

Her birthday! Today she was thirteen.

"She also said your dad wants to give Skype another try today if you're willing."

Every ache and strain seemed to weigh on Twig at once. She was so tired.

Mrs. Murley squeezed her shoulder. "Have a shower first. Keely can wait a bit longer."

Twig nodded. Casey slipped her hand in Twig's and fixed her big brown eyes on her face. "Last night, Mandy tried to eat the frosting I picked for your birthday cake. She said it didn't matter," she leaned in to whisper conspiratorially, "'cause you were gone. Janessa cried. Regina said it was nice knowing you and at least we could bake the cake and eat it anyway, but then she started crying too."

Twig smiled. She hugged Casey and almost started crying herself.

• • •

Twig settled in Mr. Murley's padded office chair. She'd let Mrs. Murley comb her clean, wet hair, as though she were just a little girl. Keely had called again while she was in the shower. As she'd rinsed away the residue of the battle in the forest, Twig had thought of Daddy—and of Ben, out in the stable getting to know Mr. Murley, probably feeling strange taking care of unicorns with him instead of with his father, probably missing his father more than ever and wishing Darian could've been there to see Dagger's nightmarish leadership of the island herd come to an end.

Twig wheeled the chair in front of the open laptop. "Hi, Daddy." She made herself look right at him this time, and she spoke loud and clear.

"Hi, baby. Happy birthday."

"Thank you." There was a melancholy silence, and Twig

suspected he was thinking how he wanted to say something about all the mess that had gotten her here, but Keely had warned him Twig didn't want to talk about that.

"I got your drawing. It's amazing. You're getting so grown up and so talented too."

"I love to draw now," she admitted. "I love you, Daddy. But I love it here. I really do."

He looked away for a second, and Twig bit her lip, struggling not to cry.

"I want you to be happy." He paused, then looked down and leafed through the stack of drawings. "I really like this one." He held up a drawing of Rain Cloud. "And this one." Casey, riding Story. "But this one is my favorite." Twig's drawing of Wonder looked strange to her now without the horn. "Is this one of the horses there?"

"That's Wonder. She's mine—for now at least. I feed her and groom her and ride her. I was there the night she was born."

The night Wonder's mother died—and so did Ben's father. Two deaths, one birth. When Twig thought of it that way, it seemed the balance was tipped in favor of the darkness of that night. But that wasn't right. That wasn't how that night felt now that Wonder was grown and strong and Ben was here and the herd was free of Dagger, and she had been a part of those wonderful mysteries that shouldn't have been able to exist.

How had all that happened? How was it possible that Daddy was holding a drawing that she was proud of? How could it be that there was so much more behind that drawing that she was even more proud of? How was it that Twig Tupper didn't need to be told now to hold her head up?

Something else had been born that night along with Wonder. Something had been born in Twig.

"When Wonder runs, she dances. And when she jumps, she floats. She's a little small for a horse. And she's different," Twig said carefully. "A rare breed."

"Sounds like just the right friend for you."

Twig nodded.

"Twig, honey, I'm coming home in two months. When I come back…"

"I know," Twig said. "I need to come home too. But, Daddy, when you come home, I want you to come here. I want you to see me here first…and then I'll go back with you."

"I can do that. I'd like to see you ride. It's hard to imagine you riding a horse, let alone one called Wonder."

"I named her."

"Of course you did." He picked up the drawing again. "From the looks of this, it's just right."

"Daddy," Twig said, "who called me Twig? First, I mean?"

"Your mom, of course. Would you rather I called you Theresa now?"

"No. Twig is just right."

•••

When she was done Skyping with Daddy, Twig had a phone call to make.

"Keely?"

"Oh. Hi, Twig. Happy birthday."

"Thank you. And thanks for the birthday presents."

Twig could almost see Keely's stunned expression through the silence on the other end of the phone. The words had come out as though she really meant them. And Twig was as surprised as Keely to realize that she actually did. She was still Twig, but she was new now. She was supposed to forgive. It had felt like such a hard thing all these months, even though she'd wanted to be different. She'd wished the Murleys would stop saying it. Wished she could scratch the verses that told her to forgive out of her Bible.

"Mrs. Murley told me you like to draw. I didn't know you could draw, Twig."

"That's okay. I didn't either."

Twig turned the box of colored pencils over in her free hand. They rolled gently inside—ninety-six colors.

"I thought you might like to try some colors now. The lady at the art store told me those are the best kind."

"I can't wait to try them. Um…can I talk to Corey?"

"Corey? I don't know. He—he doesn't know what to say."

"He doesn't have to say anything. Just put him on."

Keely let out a long sigh. Then there was silence. A moment later, breathing again.

"Corey?"

There was a choking sound.

"I forgive you, Corey. And if Emily doesn't, well, she should. Anyone can tell you're sorry."

The voice on the other end of the line shook. It

stopped and started. Finally Corey squeaked out, "Happy birthday."

"Thanks."

After she'd said good-bye to her stepfamily, Twig sank onto the couch. She picked up the envelope Mrs. Murley had set with her presents. She slid a finger under the flap. It was a plain white envelope, and inside it Twig found plain, lined paper, folded to look like a card. Twig frowned. The lines were blank. But when she turned it over, there was a heart, carefully drawn and filled in with a black pen. "Happy Birthday" was penned neatly above it. "From Mom." Twig opened the makeshift card. "I love you, Twig," it said in great big letters. Then underneath, in cramped cursive, "I don't know what else to say."

Beneath those words, the empty blue lines had bled and run together. Twig let her own tears fall among the smudged ink. She let everything blur together.

The door opened, and she heard the distinct *pat-pat* of Casey's stockinged feet. Casey snuggled up beside her.

"I'm glad you came back. I'm glad you came here."

"Me too," Twig said.

Mrs. Murley peeked in the door, which Casey had left halfway open. She sat down on the other side of Twig and wrapped her arm around her.

"Hey," Regina whispered from the doorway.

Behind Regina, Taylor protested in her own whisper and tried to drag Regina back.

"Thanks for bringing us a real wild boy."

"Regina!" Taylor said, no longer in a whisper.

But Mrs. Murley laughed a soft, tired laugh.

"Just kidding, Mrs. M. He's Mr. Murley's nephew and that makes him family, right?"

"Right." Mrs. Murley extended her arm to pull Regina and Taylor onto the couch.

Then the door flew the rest of the way open and Janessa came in with her mouth pressed into a deliberate frown. But her eyes were dancing as she said, "Is this where the birthday party is? How come I wasn't invited?"

Mandy entered after her. "There's chocolate cake," she said with her trademark scowl. "Everyone knows how you like chocolate."

Ben stood in the doorway. His cloak was off, but something intangible billowed out of him. He carried himself with the confidence of someone who'd tamed the fiercest of wild unicorns, yet he reminded Twig of when she'd first come here—a glimmer of contentment in his eyes, a flash of fear that it wouldn't last.

Was he thinking about Terracornus? About Merrill's note?

Mr. Murley came up behind Ben and put his hands on his shoulders. "What's all this silliness? I'm sorry, Ben. There are entirely too many girls in this house."

Twig smiled. "I heard something about cake."

They all tumbled out of the office and to the table, yanking each other back and laughing all the way.

Ben ate his first piece of chocolate cake ever—his first piece of chocolate anything. And then he ate three more pieces and smiled triumphantly at Twig, who'd only managed to stuff down two and a half.

Indy and Wonder were still too tired to ride, but that night Twig and Ben let them out for a stretch. Everyone watched the two unicorns—father and daughter—dance, white and silver against the dark of night, leaping like the blink of starlight.

A sliver of moon lit up the still, clear sky, and the island's gentle breeze breathed a sigh of relief; it whispered through the cedars, *You belong to us, Twig, you and your Wonder. We are waiting, waiting for something even more wonderful to happen.*

No howling, no hunting tonight. Twig dared to imagine the rest of the herd joining Indy and Wonder, dancing and not hunting. The last free herd, the unicorns of Lonehorn Island, becoming the wonder they were supposed to be.

Wonder Light
Discussion Questions

1. Lonehorn Island is full of secrets and surrounded by rumors that turn out to be only partly true. How is Lonehorn Island like Twig and the other girls of Island Ranch?

2. Though Keely bought Twig new clothes, Twig chooses to wear her old clothes instead. Why do you think Twig does this?

3. Why do you think the Murleys give each girl a pony to care for? Do you have a pet? What have you learned from having a pet? If you don't have a pet, what do you think it would be like to have an animal that needs a lot of care?

4. Why do you think Twig decides to forgive her step-brother, Corey? Have you ever had a hard time forgiving someone? What makes it hard to forgive?

5. Twig always wears a minibackpack under her shell. What does she keep inside? Why does Twig decide to share them with Ben?

For more discussion questions and classroom activities, visit www.sourcebooks.com/images/stories/docs/PDFS/WonderlightDiscussionQuestions.pdf.

Read on for an excerpt from

The Unicorn Thief

Coming Spring 2014
from Sourcebooks Jabberwocky

CHAPTER 1

THE UNICORN'S NOSTRILS FLARED at the thief in warning. Her breath came out in puffs of outrage, a visible vapor in the crisp night air. The mare's deadly horn glinted in the light of the lantern, but the thief stayed calm. He held out his hand, palm down. Then he took the tiny instrument from his pocket, held it to his lips, and began to play.

The flattened ears perked up and turned toward the sound. He'd practiced this song, refined it even more, he believed, than the great Darian ever had. His fingers danced over the holes as he blew, making music to lull the powerful Night Spark. To bring her completely under his control.

Darian, the great herder, was a man of many secrets, and this was one of them. The thief's throat tightened around his song, his heart caught in the clench of regret. Would Westland ever see Darian again? Would he? It was too easy to succumb to such dark thoughts while on castle grounds, especially here, in the royal stables.

The thief fitted Night Spark with a halter and led her out of the stall. He could hear the boots of the guards on the cobblestone outside, pacing in a steady, serious rhythm. Alert, strong. Nothing but the queen's best to guard her best.

Those guards would have a hard time explaining this. It was too bad, but it had to be done. The thief guided Night Spark through the secret opening in the back wall of the stable and into the shaft of darkness—Darian's passageway. Night Spark shuffled, eyelids drooping, as though she were sleepwalking. The thief slid the hidden panel shut and disappeared with the unicorn into the underground maze.

Chapter 2

TWIG BENT TO PUT the last plate in the dishwasher, and Ben scooped a blob of frosting off of it. He licked his finger. Twig made a face. She picked up the box of detergent and showed Ben how to open it.

Ben sniffed the citrusy detergent scent—too hard. He sneezed, and his shaggy brown hair flew into his eyes.

"I still don't understand," Ben said between sneezes. "How does this stuff get the dishes clean?"

Twig grinned. "Watch." She poured the detergent into the dishwasher, then shut the door and turned the dial. Ben's eyes widened. He knelt down, ear to the dishwasher door.

"Water!"

Ben had been raised in another world—Terracornus, land of the unicorns. He'd spent much of his life here on

Lonehorn Island, in the Earth Land, as he called it, but he'd never seen modern technology. Until the Murleys had come to Lonehorn Island and built Island Ranch—a home, pony ranch, and informal school for six troubled girls—the island had been abandoned.

"It's a machine with a motor, like the truck, only it runs on electricity. The same stuff that powers the lights in here."

"It pumps water over the dishes?"

"I guess so. It sprays them."

Ben listened for a moment, then threw open the door to the cupboard under the sink, an eager, searching look in his brown eyes. "The water comes from under here."

Twig turned on the faucet. "It's all connected."

"Amazing."

He pulled on the dishwasher door, trying to open it, but the handle wasn't visible under the matching panel across the top of the machine, and he kept missing the spot.

Twig bit her lip. Should she ask him now? If not now, when? She couldn't wait any longer. In just a couple months, her dad would come and take her home, away from the island. "Ben?"

"Hm?"

Twig pressed in and pulled out, unlatching and opening the machine a crack for him.

He peeked inside. "It stopped," he muttered with a frown.

"I was thinking, since I explained something to you, maybe you could explain something to me."

"Sure." He closed the door and started turning the dial every which-way. *Heavy wash, light wash, super soak, dry.* "It dries them too?"

Twig let out an exasperated breath and cranked the dial to the *off* position. She stood in front of the machine, blocking his view.

Ben rose, brow creased. "What?"

Twig took the note from her pocket. The one Ben had dropped back in Terracornus, before they'd killed Dagger, the blood-thirsty unicorn who'd led the island's herd to attack the ranch. Dagger had been determined to kill Twig's unicorn, Wonder, whom she'd raised from birth.

Ben had tried to hide the note from her, but in his haste, he'd dropped it, and she'd slipped it into her pocket. She hadn't had time to read it until they were safe back at the ranch. And then there'd been so much going on—finding out that Ben was a long-lost relative of the Murleys; Twig's thirteenth birthday, which she almost hadn't lived to see; Skyping her dad, who was in the army and deployed overseas, and talking to him for the first time in a year. It was hard to believe everything that had happened the last few days. It was hard to believe that after all they'd done, their work wasn't over. It was only just beginning.

Twig pressed the note against her jeans, flattening the crumpled paper. She held it out. "What's going on, Ben?"

"How'd you get that?" Ben snatched it out of her hands and stuffed it in his own pocket.

"You dropped it. What does it mean?"

Ben crossed his arms over the too-big T-shirt he'd borrowed from Mr. Murley. "It's nothing. Nothing that I can do anything about."

"Merrill said—"

"Merrill's wrong."

"Fine. Merrill's wrong. You can still tell me what he meant. What's going on in Terracornus?"

"The same old problems."

Twig put on her best "Merrill" voice—gruff, yet

warm—and quoted his note. "'It's worse than I feared here. As soon as we've dealt with Dagger you must come to Westland. For the sake of all unicorns, all Terracornus, you must appeal to the queen.' That's what it says. Sounds like more than the same old problems to me." Twig had the cryptic phrase, written by their friend and old herder, Merrill, memorized. A friend of Ben's father, Darian, Merrill had come to the island to help Twig learn to ride Wonder, and teach her to wield a short sword and handle a bow.

"But it *is* the same. There's always war in Terracornus. Merrill wants me to appeal to the queen to step down and put a democratic process back in place, so that Westland can be an example to all the other lands. He thinks Westland can be a reminder to all Terracornus of how things were meant to be."

"Can it?"

"It used to be." Abruptly, Ben's expression hardened. "But it doesn't matter. There's nothing I can do about it."

"Why does Merrill think you can, then?"

"The Queen knew my father well. He was the greatest herder in Westland, an important man. But she's changed.

The herders have been disbanded. Everything's changed. I cannot influence the queen. Not now, not ever."

• • •

Ben gathered up the books he'd just finished and carried the armful back to the bookshelf in the living room. He carefully slid each one back into place, then stood back and studied the shelves. So many books! So much he didn't know. After nearly a week at the ranch, he was beginning to wonder if he'd ever understand the way this world worked.

You have to go back to Terracornus. You have to go back to the queen. Merrill kept saying it, and now he had Twig saying it too.

What was he supposed to do? Going back there would mean turning his back on the herd. If he went to the castle, he might never return to the island—and for what? To talk to a ruler who cared nothing for what a herder had to say?

"Ben?" Mr. Murley called from the entryway. He sounded out of breath.

Ben ran to the front door.

Mr. Murley stood in the doorway, boots on, face flushed

under the hood of his jacket. Under the cover of the porch, he pushed the hood back, and rainwater spilled over his shoulders. "It's Indy."

Acknowledgments

I wrote my first book in a storage closet. It smelled like crayons and Play-Doh, and it was one of my favorite places to be, scribbling on stacks of paper my dad had brought home from work. Pages that were used on one side, still perfectly good for us kids. But when I told my mom I wanted to make a book to take to kindergarten for show-and-tell, she gave me brand-new paper and helped me fold and staple it.

My mom taught me to read and write. She taught me to love making things, and to make the things that I loved.

And so I made books.

My husband married this crazy dreamer, this maker of books. He supported me and defended my dream. Jason, you're my hero, even without a cape or a sword.

My children listened and read and demanded more.

They laughed and cried with me and rubbed my shoulders and made me coffee. Such beloved sharers of stories!

My friend Byron gave me the idea to write a book about unicorns, and so many other friends and family members believed in me and were here to lend a hand when life got hectic and deadlines loomed.

Debra E. Davies of Davies Arabians, a generous friend and a horsewoman to the heart, read and gave me helpful suggestions.

My editor, Aubrey Poole, understood Twig and Wonder. Thanks, Aubrey, for your encouragement, insight, and advocacy for this book.

When I began writing Twig's story, I shared her broken heart. Now I share her wonder. Lord, how you have blessed me! "For you are great and do wondrous things; you alone are God." (Psalm 86:10)

About the Author

R.R. Russell lives with her family in the Pacific Northwest. She grew up traveling the world as an army brat and now travels the country as a coach with a nonprofit judo club. She loves to read and draw, and like Twig, once spent a lot of time sketching unicorns. Visit her website at www.RRRussellauthor.com.

ROSE
Holly Webb

How would you know if you were special?

Mr. Fountain's grand mansion is a world away from the dark orphanage Rose has left behind. The gleaming, golden house is practically overflowing with sparkling magic—she can feel it. And though Rose has always wanted to be an ordinary girl with an ordinary life, she realizes she may possess a little bit of magic herself.

But when orphans begin mysteriously disappearing, Rose is put to the test. Can she find the missing children before it's too late?

ROSE AND THE LOST PRINCESS

Holly Webb

Not all magic is used for good…

Rose's whole life has changed in a matter of weeks. She's gone from being a lonely orphan to a magician's apprentice, though she's learned that power comes at a price. Even Rose's friends don't seem to trust her anymore, especially when rumors of dark magic begin to swirl through the city.

Then the country's beloved princess vanishes, and the king asks Rose for her help. She must find the missing princess and put a stop to the evil magician behind the kidnapping…before all is lost.

THE NINJA LIBRARIANS: THE ACCIDENTAL KEYHAND

Jen Swann Downey

An overdue library book can change your life. (So can a pet mongoose.)

When Dorrie and her brother Marcus chase Moe—an unusually foul-tempered mongoose—into the janitor's closet of their local library, they make an astonishing discovery: the headquarters of a secret society of ninja librarians. That's right—sword-swinging, karate-chopping, crime-fighting warrior librarians.

Their mission: protect those whose words have gotten them into trouble, anywhere in the world and at any time in history.

Petrarch's Library is an amazing, jumbled, time-traveling secret base that can dock anywhere there's trouble, like the Spanish Inquisition, or ancient Greece, or…Passaic, New Jersey. Dorrie would love nothing more than to join the society, fighting injustice with a real sword! But when a traitor surfaces, she and Marcus are prime suspects. Can they clear their names before the only passage back to the twenty-first century closes forever?